THE LIGHT THAT REMAINS

STORIES

LYSE CHAMPAGNE

Enfield & Wizenty
(an imprint of Great Plains Publications)
233 Garfield Street
Winnipeg, MB R3G 2MI
www.greatplains.mb.ca

Great Plains Publications gratefully acknowledges the financial support provided for its publishing program by the Government of Canada through the Canada Book Fund; the Canada Council for the Arts; the Province of Manitoba through the Book Publishing Tax Credit and the Book Publisher Marketing Assistance Program; and the Manitoba Arts Council.

Design & Typography by Relish New Brand Experience
Printed in Canada by Friesens

LIBRARY AND ARCHIVES CANADA CATALOGUING IN PUBLICATION

Champagne, Lyse, author
    The light that remains / Lyse Champagne.

Short stories.
Issued in print and electronic formats.

ISBN 978-1-927855-40-9 (paperback).--ISBN 978-1-927855-41-6 (epub).--
ISBN 978-1-927855-42-3 (mobi)

    I. Title.

PS8605.H35I5L54 2016   C813'.6   C2015-908670-I
                                           C2015-908671-X

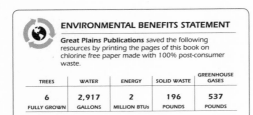

ENVIRONMENTAL BENEFITS STATEMENT

Great Plains Publications saved the following resources by printing the pages of this book on chlorine free paper made with 100% post-consumer waste.

TREES	WATER	ENERGY	SOLID WASTE	GREENHOUSE GASES
6	2,917	2	196	537
FULLY GROWN	GALLONS	MILLION BTUs	POUNDS	POUNDS

Environmental impact estimates were made using the Environmental Paper Network Paper Calculator 3.2. For more information visit www.papercalculator.org.

Canadä

FSC
www.fsc.org
MIX
Paper from
responsible sources
FSC® C016245

For all those whose stories have never been told

Is it so small a thing
To have enjoy'd the sun,
To have lived light in the spring,
To have loved, to have thought, to have done...

MATTHEW ARNOLD
FROM THE HYMN OF EMPEDOCLES

MAPS OF EUROPE

All things are bound in closest unison,
Throughout the world, by many a mystic thread.
The flower and love, the breeze and reverie,
Nature and man, and things alive and dead,
Are all akin, and bound in harmony
Throughout the world, by many a mystic thread.

ARSHAG TCHOBANIAN

Gesaria, June 15, 1914.

MY DEAREST SISTER,

The map of Europe hangs at the front of the class, as it does every Monday morning, but instead of staring at France like I usually do, at the star that marks Paris, and imagining Papa at the Café Métropolitain, writing a poem or arguing politics with his friends (without a thought to the family he has left behind), I keep glancing at the edge of the map, at the uncoloured patch that is Anatolia.

How far are you from us now? Are you close enough to the mountain that you can reach out and touch it? If the railway had been built, the one that almost bankrupted Grandfather Stepanian, you'd already be far away from us, your face pressed against the train window, your eyes wide with everything you were taking in. It's of little consolation that you are still so close, that it will take you many days to reach the station at Ulukişla.

When I went to help you dress this morning, as you had asked me to, I found you standing at the window, still in your nightdress, your hair loose, the morning light on your face.

I paused in the doorway for a moment. As long as you didn't turn around, we had time. And time is all I wanted.

You waved at someone in the courtyard and stepped away from the window. I slipped behind the screen before you turned around, before you realized I was there. I wasn't ready. I would never be ready.

You gathered the dark clothes Mama had left for you – the ones that were supposed to make you look like a man, that were supposed to keep you safe, the clothes I had fancied myself wearing, mounted on a fine horse, a Karabakh like the one Papa rode when he began his journey away from us.

When you crossed the room and dropped the clothes in front of the looking glass, you were so close I could've touched you. I was sure you would hear me breathing on the other side of the screen.

I should've shown myself then or greeted you at least, so you could've asked me what I was doing there, spying on you like a servant girl, so we could've laughed about it as we sorted through the clothes together. But I couldn't bring myself to move or speak. I watched as you slipped into the black cotton shirt and the pantaloons, as you puzzled over the ties on the loose jacket. As you braided your hair and coiled it under an old cap of Papa's.

Mihran strode into the room from the other doorway and you showed off your disguise, turning slowly in front of him, your arms outstretched, your hands lost in the long sleeves, and when he knelt down to tie the pantaloons around your ankles, I couldn't bear the way he looked up at you, the way his hand lingered on the back of your leg.

You were so intent on each other you never saw me step away from the screen. Never saw me leave.

How could you marry Mihran and move so far away from us, so far away from me, when we were supposed to marry brothers and live under the same roof? (I can't even be mad at Mihran because he had brothers and now they're all dead.) It's unfair, I know, to hold you to a promise we made years ago, before we knew anything about marriage or the misery of living under someone else's roof.

I'm sorry I wasted the time you had set aside for us to be together. I was counting on riding in the wagon with you as far as the city gate but Ovsanna was crying, Dalita and Tsangali were clutching at my skirts, and I couldn't leave Mama standing there, her hands tucked under her apron, holding the sadness in her belly like an unborn baby.

When you reach the farm tonight, you'll find the letter I slipped into your bag before it was loaded onto the wagon. I didn't want you to spend your first night away from home without words of mine next to your heart. For words are what we've shared the most, aren't they? Words whispered in bed, shouted at play, spoken on the way to school. Words and the absence of words, for we had to learn to be quiet once we moved into Grandmother's house, where our words were greeted with scorn.

Our dear teacher lets me scribble furiously on this, the first day of our separation. She didn't wait for me to hang the map this morning so it clattered to the floor twice before she could balance it on the hooks properly. I will stop now and help her with the little ones.

May God keep you safe on the long road to Ulukişla.

Your loving Shoushan

Saraycik, June 15, 1914.

My dearest Shoushan,

I'm sitting at the table by the window, where Mama used to write to Papa before they were married. The farmyard is dark but there is an afterglow on the mountain, the snow the same delicate pink it was that last evening we spent with Papa. Remember how we stood on our balcony, transfixed, while he explained how snow could still reflect light after the sun had set? I can't recall his explanation, only the sound of his voice in the darkness, the smell of his French cigarette. We stayed there, long after the rosiness had faded, while Papa described Paris and the wonderful life we would have when we joined him there.

Are you standing on Grandmother's balcony as I write this, leaning over the railing in that careless way you have, admiring the same afterglow on the mountain? I can't believe that Mount Argeus now stands between us, as will other mountains we have never seen, with names we vaguely remember from our geography lessons.

The letter you slipped into my bag is propped against the sill, your beautiful script a balm for my sand-scratched eyes. You cannot imagine how grateful I was to find it after the emotions of the day, after all those hours on the road. You are not the only one who feels bereft, little sister. Yes, I have a husband now and the togetherness that marriage brings but I had to leave five of you at once. And as much as I love Ovsanna, Tsangali, and little Dalita, my heart aches for you the most. I miss Mama too, of course, which is a different kind of ache.

The road was interminable, stretching across the plain, with the foothills and the mountains ahead of us, the walls of Gesaria behind us. For a long time, we seemed trapped between those two points, as if the horses were plodding in place, as if the wheels of the wagon were spinning in the sand. I wonder what Papa was thinking, when he trod the same road, setting out in search of a better life for our family, a life that will no longer include me.

Remember when we first laid eyes on Mihran after he was hired by Mr. Nazarian? How we watched from Grandmother's balcony as he loaded carpets onto the wagon with our cousins? You made fun of his clothes, his hair, his sad, scrawny face.

It was working in Uncle Jivan's bookshop after school that put me in regular contact with him. He came in on his afternoon off, to leaf through the biology and anatomy books he couldn't afford. I watched him for weeks but he never showed any interest. Or so I thought. Then one day he slipped a note in a book before returning it to me and we exchanged notes thereafter, not wanting anyone to know of our interest in each other.

I don't know why Grandmother allowed me to marry Mihran when everyone except Uncle Jivan was against it. Perhaps she is so disillusioned with Papa she no longer cares what happens to his children. Mihran is accepted here, at the farm. No one cares that he is the son of a tenant farmer. No one mocks him for wanting to be a doctor.

My heart is lighter now that I know Aram will be bringing you these letters, that you will be reading them as soon as tomorrow. You will find him much changed. He is as vehement and politically-minded as Mihran, no longer the sweet, dreamy boy we used to know.

I love being here, surrounded by Mama's family. It reminds me of our house on Bahçebasi Street, the life we had before we moved in with Grandmother. I have never understood why Papa encouraged us to have opinions, to practise being European as he called it, only to leave for France without us. He could have at least arranged for us to live here, at the farm, where we would have been freer and happier. I hope Papa didn't leave us with Grandmother so she would keep sending him money in France, as Uncle Hagop has so cruelly claimed.

Take heart, little sister, we will not be apart for long. As soon as we reach Zmurnia, we will finalize the arrangements for you to study at the American Collegiate Institute. With our dear teacher's recommendation, I'm sure we will have no problem securing a place for you there.

Auntie Lusine, Auntie Yevkeneh, Armine and Manishag and our cousins' wives send their love. They are clamouring for me to join their game of *belotte*. They have obviously forgotten how hopeless I am at cards.

Missing you too much already,
Khatoun

Gesaria, June 16, 1914.

Dearest Khatoun,

How surprised we were when we returned from school and found Aram drinking coffee in the courtyard with Mama, your two letters on the table between them. While the girls swarmed over Aram, looking for sweets, I moved to a quiet corner to savour your letters. I hadn't finished the first one when the girls crowded around me, pulling at the pages with their sticky hands, their mouths full of candy, demanding that I read it to them.

They ran off when I opened the second letter, the one you had written to me, and I was able to read it in peace. Next time, I hope you'll write more about what you saw on the road, that you won't claim, as Papa often did, that travelling is more tedious than glamorous. How can it be tedious to move over another patch of earth, to pass a tree you've never seen before, to view the mountain from a different angle?

Aram is different. I couldn't believe the way he challenged Uncle Hagop on the Constitution, on the need for an Armenian homeland. Uncle Jivan could have helped him out but didn't. He wanted to sing and Aram to accompany him. I am listening to them as I write this, the *duduk* making me homesick for the farm, for all the summers we spent there as children. Words can't convey the emptiness in my heart.

Your loving Shoushan

Incesu, June 16, 1914.

My dearest sister,

We are covered in red dust. It clings to our clothes, our skin, our eyelashes. Seeps into our nostrils, settles between our teeth like crumbs. Every muscle and bone in my body aches (Mihran likes to rattle off the names of these muscles and bones, as he has studied them in his anatomy book). We are lucky to be sitting at all. We meet many who travel on foot, with heavy burdens on their backs or leading donkeys buckling under the weight of their wares.

I love the freedom dressing like a man affords me. When we stop to water the horses or chat with someone on the road, no one pays me the slightest attention. I am simply one of Mr. Nazarian's helpers, a young man of no consequence.

When we encountered a broken-down wagon near Incesu, Mr. Nazarian ignored the owner's pleas but Mihran insisted we stop. Since the wagon had to be unloaded for the wheel to be repaired, Mihran argued quietly with Mr. Nazarian that I had to help, that I had to behave like a man at all times. It was hard work but I was happy to participate, to stand on solid ground again after all that swaying.

We are staying with Auntie Hasmig's brothers, in the gloomy house where she grew up. Incesu is not as beautiful as I expected. It is built against a backdrop of sheer rock, as our Auntie has always described it, but the edges are broken and the rock face looks like a ruin. The houses are scattered over hilly ground which makes them seem lopsided and comical.

Her brothers wept when they read her letter. Can you imagine anyone weeping over Auntie Hasmig? Maybe if Uncle Hagop allowed her more contact with her family, she would be less sour. I cannot imagine writing to you only once a year!

I'm feeling homesick. Two days ago, I watched the girls chasing each other in the courtyard, laughing and waving up at me. Yesterday, I was at the farm, surrounded by Mama's boisterous family. But from now on, I will live among strangers, walk down streets I do not recognize, pray in a church that is not mine. Your letter is my talisman and I keep it close to my heart, inside the black shirt, where I can feel it shift against my skin as the wagon sways. I intend to read it every night (even if Mihran teases me about it) until we arrive in Zmurnia, until I can collect the letters which will have accumulated for me there. I hope you are writing to me every day, as you promised.

I wake up often in the night. I can't get used to my husband's snoring, as vociferous as his opinions. I miss our room. What I would give to hear the girls giggle under their blankets. To feel your restless body next to mine, your exuberance untainted by sleep.

Your loving Khatoun

Gesaria, June 17, 1914.

Dearest Khatoun,

There was a letter from Papa today, a long letter he obviously intended us to receive before your wedding, which Grandmother opened, although it was addressed to Mama, and read aloud after supper. He also sent poems, which she didn't read, and so we were spared Auntie Hasmig's contempt, and a separate letter and package for you which Grandmother didn't open so your marriage must've changed your status in her eyes.

Papa returned to the store where he bought Mama's wedding dress twenty years ago and chose something you could wear with the dress to make it your own, not that we know what it is, since Mama won't let us open the package.

Papa should have come to your wedding instead of sending some finery from Paris, however lovely it might be. He should have seen how beautiful you looked in Mama's dress, how European. The dress is still hanging in our room. The girls like to hide under the skirt and whisper and giggle together and I sleep with it at night, the lace bodice against my face, my arms around its silky fullness.

Both you and Mama wore that dress to marry a man of your choosing but I'm afraid I won't be so lucky. Grandmother is already looking for a husband for me, less than a week after you and Mihran exchanged your vows. Several mothers visited today, a veritable procession, and after they left, I was scolded me for being sullen and clumsy.

Krikor came to our quarters this evening to ask Mama if he could copy Papa's latest poems. "I have the greatest respect for my uncle's gift," he assured Mama when she hesitated. Respect? When has Krikor ever shown us respect?

I miss you so much. Ovsanna climbs into bed with me at night, Tsangali sits next to me at dinner, and Mama prepares all my favourite foods. But how can I eat or sleep when you're travelling away from us, when I might be married off to a stranger at any moment?

If only you were in Zmurnia already, my future could be decided more quickly. Of course, by the time you read this, you will be in Zmurnia since I can only send this letter to Mihran's uncle's address there.

Your soon to be sacrificed sister,
Shoushan

Dörtyol, June 17, 1914.

Dear Shoushan,

We had a terrible incident on the road which you must not mention to Mama or she will never allow you to travel to the station at Ulukişla. Our wagon was damaged in a rock slide this morning and Mr. Nazarian was barely able to bring the horses under control. Before we could get underway again, two brigands appeared, brandishing swords (Mihran figures they triggered the rock slide).

Mr. Nazarian drew a pistol and fired it in the air and the thieves rode off, their swords still aloft.

Afterwards I was sick to my stomach with fear (you would have been braver, I'm sure) and every time I heard horses behind us, I thought the thieves were coming back. When Mihran directed Mr. Nazarian to a smaller, rougher track, I became even more anxious. If we were not safe on the main road, why were we taking a chance on a less travelled one?

We soon came upon a large, shallow lake, its edges thick with reeds. It was not until the wagon stopped rumbling over the uneven terrain that I heard the squawking and the beating of wings. Flamingoes, hundreds of them, burst out of the reeds. They seemed clumsy at first, dangling their skinny legs over the water, but grew more graceful as they pulled upwards. They circled above us, their black-tipped wings spread wide, and swooped down again and again, in a dizzying blur of pink and white.

I've enclosed several feathers for you and the girls.

Your loving Khatoun

Gesaria, June 22, 1914.

Dearest Khatoun,

When Mr. Nazarian returned, he never mentioned the rock slide or the thieves. He must've had the wagon repaired in Ulukişla because I couldn't see any evidence of damage. It's only because I've read the letter you entrusted to him that I know any different. I'm grateful that you're both safe and travelling the rest of the way by train.

Mama cried as she read your letter although you didn't tell her everything. The further you move away from us, the sadder she becomes. Every time she cries, Grandmother scolds her, reminding her that you are a *harss* now, that you no longer belong to us but to your husband's family. A strange and cruel comment, given that Mihran has no family, that his parents and brothers were killed in Adana five years ago.

I have tried to imagine them at your wedding reception, these young men who should have been your brothers-in-law. Awkward in their good clothes, afraid to ask anyone to dance. Heaping their plates with lamb and pilaf, drinking too much *raki*. And me standing to one side, trying to decide which of them I would marry.

Meanwhile, you'll be pleased to know that Grandmother is not seeking a husband for me but a bride for Krikor, which will keep her busy since he's the eldest son of an eldest son and can't marry just anybody. By the time she turns her attention to me again, I should be safely out of reach, behind the walls of the American Collegiate Institute.

Krikor doesn't want to get married any more than I do. He wants to study in Europe, like Papa did, and even wrote to him to seek his advice (which explains his sudden interest in our father's poetry). Not that Uncle Hagop will ever be swayed by anything Papa might say – we both know how he despises our father and his European education. I pity the poor girl who marries our cousin as I would not wish Auntie Hasmig and Uncle Hagop on anyone.

Our dear teacher invited us to dinner. We met her brother Levon and her Aunt Lousaper, who raised them both. Her brother stared at me all through dinner, which made me uncomfortable, and left before the meal was over. Krikor later told me that Levon Tsulikian teaches at his school and is heavily involved in politics.

A friend of Papa's in Paris stopped in Gesaria on his way to visit his family (he at least visits his). He brought us a parcel from Papa with letters for everyone, a book of Armenian poems by expatriates (with two of Papa's poems, in Armenian and French), some Swiss chocolate, dolls for the girls (although Ovsanna no longer plays with them), and scarves for Mama and me. Mine is a lovely mix of blues and greens and I'm wearing it as I write this.

I've been helping Uncle Jivan and Auntie Azniv with the bookstore after school. Taking your place, as I have at school and at home. I miss you terribly when I'm there, seeing you in every corner, your nose in a book, oblivious to the rest of the world (and any customers requiring assistance although book lovers seem to not require any).

This morning I hung the map of Europe for Miss Tsulikian so she wouldn't have to struggle with it like she did last week and found it heavier than I remembered. And since the rings don't quite line up with the hooks, I almost dropped it too.

Your loving Shoushan

Zmurnia, June 23, 1914.

Dearest sister,

We reached Zmurnia late yesterday afternoon. I am sitting on the floor of our flat, surrounded by trunks. When Mihran left to find a *gradaran*, I stopped unpacking and reread all the letters that were waiting for us when we arrived.

I was moved by Papa's poems, especially the one about the coming and going of the light. I could feel his longing for home. Although he was describing a park in Paris, I recognized the public garden at the end of our street where Azniv used to take us as children, before she married Uncle Jivan. You were always playing in the fountain there, getting your hair and dress wet, no matter how often you were scolded for it. It's that fountain I see in the poem, the carvings worn away, moss growing in every crevice, the light on the water as golden and delicate as the illuminations in Uncle Jivan's antique books.

I have opened Papa's parcel and cannot wait to show you the beautiful shawl he sent me, made of the same Alençon lace as the bodice of Mama's dress. I still think of it as her dress but now I have a shawl that will remind me of it and yet be my own. I have already written to Papa to thank him for his thoughtful gift.

Our flat is in the Armenian quarter, near the church where Mama and Papa were married twenty years ago. I can see the steeple from our window. Last night, we had dinner with Mihran's aunt, her husband and their children.

Their youngest, Apkar, is keen to show us around. He took us down to the quays this morning, past the American Collegiate Institute where his sister Siroun teaches. It lightened my heart to picture you living and studying there, just a few blocks from our flat.

The ships were taller and broader than I expected and noisier too. You would not believe how loudly they creak as they shift in the water and bump up against the stone wharf. We watched as carpets rolled in burlap were hoisted over our heads and dumped on the deck of a ship bound for America. On the next ship, which was flying a British flag, the men were loading bales of wool and silk. Apkar told us how the cargo and the smell would change later in the summer, as the shipments of figs, raisins, and tobacco moved through the port.

There was so much noise around us, so much movement, that I felt dizzy. I saw my first tramcar and two automobiles (which finally drew Mihran's interest) amidst the usual mix of wagons and carriages, camels, horses and donkeys. Itinerant sellers offered us syrup, tea, raisins, and pumpkin seeds.

As we moved away from the ships, we saw more of the bay, the hills on the other side. The water was a deep, mysterious blue, like the stones in Mama's lapis necklace. We could smell freshly baked bread, grilling meat, and the rose petals heaped in baskets at every street corner.

We passed hotels and cafés, banks, shipping companies, two theatres, one cinema and many foreign consulates, including the French one where Papa had his papers stamped. As we moved away from the port, the area became residential, the stone houses three stories high, with ornate doorways, bay windows and wrought iron balconies. We followed the houses all the way to the Point and took a horse-drawn tram back. I got used to sitting with complete strangers on the train but this was more intimate, as Europeans look you in the eye when they speak to you.

On the quays I heard Greek, Turkish, French, and Armenian, and languages I did not recognize. You'd think we were in Constantinople! The signs were in Greek and French, which surprised me. There are apparently more Greeks here than in Athens.

As we passed the Café de Paris, which was quite large and imposing, I wondered if Papa had spent time there while waiting for his ship to sail. If he had written a letter or a poem at one of the tables I saw, his eyes on the waters of the bay.

We stopped at the bazaar to buy *lavash*, *panir*, and *sarma* for our dinner. We invited Apkar to stay and then we had visitors later on, two men Mihran had met at the gradaran. They brought raki which they drank from the bottle as we had not unpacked our glasses. They are still here as I write this, arguing loudly.

I will send you more descriptions of Zmurnia soon. Please let me know the date you receive this letter so I can figure how long it takes for my mail to reach home.

Khatoun

Zmurnia, June 29, 1914.

Dearest Shoushan,

Yesterday we went to the church where Mama and Papa were married twenty years ago. As I thought about them, the vows they exchanged there, the family they created, I felt less lonely, less bereft.

Apkar continues to take us around his beautiful city even though Mihran slips away at the first opportunity. Today we went up on the *Asansör* to admire Zmurnia from above. This elevator connects two streets, at the top and bottom of a steep cliff. I was too excited to feel fear when the doors closed and our cage started to move up. We stepped out onto a terrace with a spectacular view of the water, the big freighters at anchor in the bay, the fishing boats and loading barges streaming into port. I imagined you beside me, leaning dangerously over the railing, pointing out our apartment building, your school, all the places you could already recognize and demanding to see the rest.

We rode the elevator back down and while Mihran went off to the gradaran to read the Armenian papers, Apkar took me to the main shopping street. You will love *la rue Franque*, little sister. It's as busy as a bazaar but with stores like we've never seen before, with glass fronts and mannequins dressed in the latest European styles. We only had time to visit one of these department stores, Xenopoulos, and it reminded me of the postcard Papa sent us of a *magasin à rayons* in Paris. I could not believe the displays, the merchandise available, the women who milled around me. The way they were dressed, the way they moved about so much more freely than we did at home.

When we made our way back to the Armenian quarter, we found a crowd outside the gradaran. There was a bulletin taped to the inside of the window and it took us some time to get close enough to read it. It was about an assassination in Serbia. When Mihran finally emerged from within, he was pale and subdued.

I don't recognize my husband, Shoushan. He was the one who wanted to live here and yet he is so miserable. Maybe he can't forget that he was here, visiting his aunt and uncle, when his family was massacred in Adana. Not that he has ever talked to me about it. I shudder at the thought of losing you in a massacre like that.

I miss you more than I can say. Hope we can send for you soon.

Your loving Khatoun

Gesaria, July 1, 1914.

My dearest Khatoun,

Forgive me for not writing for over a week. I've been crying and lamenting my fate, unwilling to set it down on paper lest it make it more real.

Levon Tsulikian wants to marry me! This is why we were invited for dinner, why the man was staring at me so. I don't understand how our teacher could have suggested me to her aunt when she knows how much I want to study at the American Collegiate Institute (which she herself recommended), how much I want to teach, how much I want to join Papa in France.

And the worst of it is that Grandmother and Uncle Hagop have entered into discussions with Lousaper Tsulikian. So now my fate lies in Grandmother's hands, just as yours did. Papa is too far away to intervene. Uncle Jivan has spoken up but when has Uncle Hagop ever listened to him? Why am I to be sacrificed in this way?

Please write and give me hope. Time is running out.

Shoushan

Zmurnia, July 6, 1914.

Dearest sister,

I know you are waiting impatiently for news about your application but I have nothing to report. Mihran has not contacted the school nor secured a position for himself. He has not even met with the merchants Uncle Hagop recommended. I know this because the envelope with the list of names, which Uncle had entrusted to me, is still sealed and in my possession.

Mihran practically lives at the gradaran. He spends money from my marriage settlement without asking me about it and won't let me hire a servant, even though his Aunt Araxie has sent several girls for my consideration. The flat is small and easy to clean and I enjoy preparing our meals but I would like the girl for company, if nothing else.

Enough about Mihran. I'm sure you want to read about Zmurnia. I have not been to the Turkish quarter up the hill, I have only seen the *infidel* part of the city, as Apkar claims the Turks call it. He took me down to the European quay yesterday evening. It was so exciting. Streets full of people, Greek music spilling out of the cafés, strings of light everywhere. The waters of the bay were black, the shadows cast by the ships, very large.

Apkar wants to take me to the cinema with his sisters but I'm waiting until you arrive so we can see our first film together.

Uncle Dikran invited us to a recital at the Armenian Club last night and was displeased when I stepped into the carriage without Mihran. Luckily, Siroun and Anoush were there to dispel the awkwardness. The Armenian Club was lively. There was much talk and laughter but also worry. About that assassination in Serbia. How it might lead to another war in the Balkans, like the one in 1912 and the one last year.

As a new bride, I shudder at all this talk of war. What will happen to Mihran? Uncle Hagop has already paid his *bedel* but the Turks could still conscript him. He will never fight for them, not after they massacred his family.

It's hard to think of war when the sky and the bay are so blue and the air is sweet with the smell of jasmine.

Khatoun

Gesaria, July 15, 1914.

Dearest Khatoun,

We have finally received the first two letters you wrote from Zmurnia. I've fixed your wonderful descriptions of the city in my mind and every night, as I wait for sleep, I imagine myself riding the Asansör and shopping on rue Franque.

The situation here remains unchanged, with Mama and Grandmother still arguing about Levon Tsulikian's proposal and Grandfather Karamanian and Uncle Bedros travelling from the farm to support Mama. I don't understand why Grandmother and Uncle Hagop favour the match when the Tsulikians are neither wealthy nor influential, when Markrid's aunt still teaches the piano and Levon and Markrid help support the household. But maybe that's the point. They let you marry the son of a tenant farmer and now they want me to marry a teacher so heavily involved in politics, he may belong to a secret society.

We may live in the family nest but we are pressed up against the sides, against the straw and twigs and feathers.

You must be so happy with your new husband, your new life. Don't forget me, sister, please.

Shoushan

Zmurnia, July 23, 1914.

My dear sweet sister,

I'm sorry that I am so far away, that I can't relieve your distress over Levon Tsulikian's proposal. Papa wouldn't want you to marry someone against your will, you know that very well, and even if he is in Paris, he is still the head of our family. I sent him a telegram this morning and I am sure Mama has already sent him several. He has to intervene.

Unfortunately, my husband's actions will only add to your distress. I have just learned that we leave tonight for Marseille on a cargo ship, *Le Général Metzinger*. His uncle knew of his plans, as did Apkar, but his aunt is as shocked as I am.

When I thought he was at the gradaran, dabbling in politics, he was out obtaining false papers, bribing agents, and arranging our passage. With all these war rumours, he had to move up the date and spend even more money. He only came to Zmurnia to book passage to France and I was sadly unaware of it.

I could stay behind, return to Gesaria, but what kind of life would I have there? As a married woman with a husband abroad, I would have to return to Grandmother's house and I cannot bear to do that. My life is with Mihran now.

The only good news I have is that my husband has secured a place for you at the American Collegiate Institute. He arranged it the first week we were here and never mentioned it to me. I guess he was afraid you would arrive before we sailed, that you would convince me to stay behind. I know you wanted to study in Zmurnia to be near me, but now you can come here to take your destiny in hand, as Mama and Papa did when they married. Mihran's aunt is ready to welcome you and has promised to send a telegram to Mama offering her help.

I am worried you will never forgive me. You were so angry when I chose to marry Mihran, when we were supposed to marry brothers and live under the same roof.

I love you, my dearest sister. My life with Mihran has not diminished this love but deepened it. Write to me care of Papa if you have the heart to write me at all.

Khatoun

Marseille, January 15, 1915.

My dearest sister,

Only seven months have passed since I left Gesaria with Mihran and yet everything has changed. I live in a strange country, you are married to a man I have never met, and the Europe that Papa has prepared us for is embroiled in a terrible war. I never thought, when I first read about the assassination in Serbia, that so many countries would get involved, that it would result in such a catastrophe.

Although the war is the main subject of conversation here, our day-to-day life has not changed much. We are so far from the front. Our fellow boarders are mostly Italian and Greek construction workers who have lived here for years. There are also two Armenian brothers from Sivas who are waiting to sail to America.

Madame Arnaud, our landlady, is kind to me. She lends me books, lets me use her bicycle and her sewing machine. Although I've learned to ride the bicycle, I'm too nervous to explore the city by myself. I realize now that if it had not been for Apkar I would not have seen much of Zmurnia either. That I am more curious than adventurous. Not like you. I remember how you begged Mama to take you to the bazaar, not to buy anything, but to escape the confines of our house, our street.

I write you letters I cannot mail because the countries we live in are at war. Not that you answered any of the letters I wrote to you after we arrived in France. Do you recall what you wrote in that letter I read at Grandfather's farm? How you wanted me to have your words next to my heart? I miss them now, the words you whispered in the darkness when we should have been asleep, in Church, when we should have been listening to the sermon. The words you scribbled furiously on that first day of our separation (I remember every word of every letter you ever wrote me). Why are you hoarding them now? Why can you not forgive me?

Mihran works long hours on the docks without complaint. He is so happy to be out of Turkey he is willing to work anywhere for anyone. He has applied to the Faculté de médecine here in Marseille, although there is no chance he will be accepted.

Papa visits every month but he is often delayed as the trains are diverted for troop movements. He is bitter and anxious, worried about you all.

I try to imagine you as a married woman, living in the same house as Markrid and her aunt. I hope Levon treats you well, that he is gentle with you and shares his thoughts.

I can hear Madame Arnaud's step on the stairs, her little dog barking (she carries him everywhere). She must have a letter from Papa for me.

Maybe this wretched war will end soon and our lives will return to normal. I love you and miss you so much.

Khatoun

Khatoun

Now that we can't write to one another, I sit down at my husband's desk and scribble these words.

I struggle with my new role of wife. Levon is reserved and awkward. Never laughs. Mama tells me to be patient, that loving someone takes time but what does she know – she and Papa were a love match and married in Zmurnia so their families couldn't intervene.

Not that I can undo what I have done. I married him in a fit of despair and must live with the consequences.

Mama and the girls visit often in spite of Grandmother's disapproval. Mama and Aunt Lousaper have become friends and so have Markrid and I. It was strange at first since she used to be our teacher but now I simply think of her as Markrid. I have never had a friend before, you were the only friend I ever wanted or needed, and I can't tell her everything, like how I really feel about her brother.

I enjoy the freedom of Aunt Lousaper's home. She's an interesting and cultured lady. She was in Constantinople, studying music with an Italian teacher there, when her brother and sister-in-law were killed and she had to return to raise Levon and Markrid. She has helped me understand why Mihran had to leave Turkey and thinks we should all leave before there are more massacres. Mama has hired a French tutor for the girls and intends to join Papa in Paris as soon as the war is over, whether he sends for her or not.

If I could mail this letter, I probably wouldn't. If you hadn't married Mihran and moved so far away, I never would've married Levon. I would still be living at home with Mama and the girls, waiting for Papa to send for us. You have ruined my life.

Shoushan

Marseille, February 18, 1915.
Dearest Shoushan,

The *mistral* has finally abated. The sky over Marseille is iridescent, the winter sunlight soft and lemony. I'm sitting in the square near our boarding house with a letter from Mama, which Uncle Hagop sent with a load of carpets he shipped through Alexandria. To have news from home was gift enough but Mama also sent a photo of the girls and one of your wedding. I will tape the pictures to the wall next to Papa's photo at the Café Métropolitain which was taken when he first arrived in Paris in 1912.

There is a box under my bed for the letters I write to you and Mama and cannot send. I reread them when I'm lonely and invent replies I might have received, full of details about your lives. I miss your long convoluted sentences, your beautiful script. Mama wrote that you seem happy enough since your marriage, that you enjoy living in Lousaper Tsulikian's house. I'm worried that she is mistaken.

Every afternoon I tutor the children of the richest Armenian merchant in Marseille. They can speak Armenian (with a lot of French mixed in) but cannot write it. The girls are eager but I have to bribe the boys to learn their Armenian letters. Their father pays me well and their mother has instructed the cook to give me food to take home. I share this food at the boarding house table and when the brothers from Sivas serve themselves, their eyes fill with tears.

The merchant's house has electricity. You press a switch on the wall to turn on the lights. The tramcars also run on electricity, from overhead cables, and there are motorcars, although less than a few months ago because petrol is being rationed. The family I work for has a motorcar and they have promised me a ride in the country this spring.

Monsieur Hagopian has two brothers who live in Montréal, Canada, and he suggested that Mihran might want to go and work for them after the war. His own sons will be going as soon as they are old enough. I have not mentioned it to Mihran because I know he would love to move to Canada and I could not bear to be farther from you than I already am.

There is an Armenian newspaper here in Marseille and at least two in Paris but they publish less frequently now because of the war. From what I have read of them, they sound just like the ones back home, agitating for the impossible, although I was happy to read Papa's poem in the last edition Mihran brought home.

I pray for the end of the war so that I can send you mail again and receive some in return.

Your loving Khatoun

Dear sister,

I knew it was a mistake to write you a letter, even if I didn't mail it. It only made me want to write to you again. How could you leave the country without taking me with you? Why didn't Mihran let me know he had secured a place for me at the Institute, so I could've travelled there before you left? So that I might have at least seen you again?

Levon has hung a map of Europe over his desk. It's a battered map he brought home from school, patched together with tape that has yellowed and buckled. I sit at his desk sometimes during the day and stare at France, the way I used to in Markrid's class. Only my eyes are on Marseille instead of Paris.

We had a map of Europe in our house, remember? It didn't roll up like the ones at school. It was an antique map Papa bought at a kiosk along the Seine. He had it framed and gave it to Mama as a wedding gift. When we first moved to Grandmother's house, Mama hung it in our quarters but soon took it down again and hid it in her trunk, wrapped in a lace tablecloth. I think she took it down because she couldn't bear to look at the distance between Gesaria and Paris, between us and Papa.

Mama gave me the map and the tablecloth when I married and I keep them at the bottom of my trunk. Levon doesn't know about the map. I'm afraid that if I show it to him, he'll hang it over his desk and make it his map, that the dream Papa had for his family will become his dream and that he too will fail to realize it.

I think of that map when Levon climbs into my bed, when he touches me the way husbands touch their wives. I fix my mind on the gilt frame, the ragged edge of the parchment, the spidery writing. The glass squealing as I drag my finger across the Mediterranean to the port of Marseille.

Shoushan

Marseille, March 24, 1915.

My darling sister,

I've been worried ever since I heard that the British and the French tried to land in Turkey last week. Mihran claims they are only interested in the Dardanelles, not our dusty town on the Anatolian plateau, but this does not reassure me. I'm glad now that the railway line through Gesaria was never built – you may be safer because of it.

I still have the letter you wrote to me before I left Gesaria. It has been folded and unfolded so many times, the edges are as limp as an old handkerchief. You filled it with every memory you had of me, of us, of our life before we moved to Grandmother's house. The stories I used to tell you, the poems we learned by heart, the songs we sang while we walked to school. All the times you strayed into an alleyway and I dragged you out again. The times we went to the bazaar by ourselves and the fortune teller you were always so eager to see.

I also think about our life together. How we gossiped on the balcony and spied on the people in the street below. How we ran around the lemon trees in the courtyard with our sisters. I remember the last Easter we were all together, you and I in our blue silk dresses, the girls in pink, as we sat on our cushions in Surb Grigor Lusavorich and listened to the church choir, to Papa's beautiful baritone. Papa never sings here. I don't know if he even attends Church. Mihran does not come with me unless I insist. And how can one insist that another believe in God?

My husband never talks about his family now. Adana, Anatolia, Turkey, the Ottoman Empire do not exist for him. He speaks only of the future. He does not want me to talk about my family either, although he is the one who has taken me away from you all. I'm miserable here but he is too drunk with his own freedom to notice. Now he wants to go to America with the two brothers from Sivas. I have not mentioned Monsieur Hagopian's brothers in Canada.

I look forward to the end of this war so we can begin to live our lives again.

Your sister who misses you so much
Khatoun

Dear Khatoun,

I don't date my letters and burn them once I finish them. As the pages flame up and disintegrate, I can see the ink lingering in the smoke. Are you also writing to me?

The British and the French are trying to invade us. Levon hopes they'll succeed and destroy what's left of the Ottoman Empire. Sounds grand doesn't it? Bringing down an empire? Until you stop to think of all the innocent people who will be crushed by the debris. Levon tried to show me what might happen on his map but my eyes were on Marseille.

Why should I care about empires or the strength of the British navy? I just want to see you again. I'm so miserable I could die.

Shoushan

Gesaria, May 21, 1915.

Dearest Khatoun,

Levon was arrested several weeks ago and may already be dead. Krikor claims that Armenian intellectuals and artists have been rounded up in other cities. We are also hearing disturbing news from the east, about deportations to Syria.

Krikor thinks we should all leave before the situation worsens, that we are wealthy enough to buy our way out of Turkey. Uncle Hagop doesn't agree. He claims his powerful connections will protect the family. Krikor isn't waiting to see who'll be proven right, he is leaving tomorrow. I don't know why he confided in me or why he offered to take a letter for you which he will mail in Alexandria. I feel guilty because neither of us has ever liked Krikor and yet he is thinking of us as he makes his preparations to leave.

I feel terrible about Levon and wish I had been a better wife, that I had made more of an effort to love him. Markrid and Aunt Lousaper are devastated and I feel like such a hypocrite when they try to console me!

I love you, dearest Khatoun, I always have. I should've rejoiced when you escaped to France instead of being so petty and selfish. If I had been the one to leave, you would've been happy for me, even if it meant you would never see me again.

Please stay safe so we can be reunited when this brutal war is over.

Your foolish and selfish sister,
Shoushan

Gesaria, June 15, 1915.

Dearest Khatoun,

Everyone is in a panic. I don't know if I will have time to finish this letter or if I will even find someone I can give it to (perhaps Mustapha Bey, that great friend of Papa's).

The town crier went down our street this morning. We have to close our businesses today and leave Gesaria within three days. Grandmother sent word that I am to travel with them, offering to take Markrid and Aunt Lousaper as well, which is a great relief. I will be going over to the house later to help with the preparations. I hope our uncles and cousins will have returned by then – we haven't seen them since they were rounded up last Friday.

I was finally able to visit Levon in prison last week. He was thinner, bruised, barely coherent. He urged me to leave Gesaria with Markrid, to ask his friend Kevork to take us across the border into Syria. I didn't have the heart to tell him Kevork was dead.

Krikor left with Aram almost three weeks ago. I'm the one who suggested they travel together. Imagine that, two cousins, one from each side of the family, escaping from all this madness, each with a letter for you.

May God keep you safe and bring us together one day soon.

Your most loving Shoushan

Montreal, June 15, 1923.

The Chairman
Armenian Relief Fund
159 Collier Street
Toronto, Ontario

Dear Sir,

I am looking for members of my family and my husband's family who were deported from Turkey in 1915. I have already written to the orphanages and refugee associations in Syria, Lebanon, Egypt, and Greece and have posted ads in Armenian newspapers in Canada, America, and Europe. All of my efforts have been unsuccessful. These relatives lived in Gesaria (Kayseri) and

Saraycik, both in Ankara Vilayet and in Zmurnia (Izmir). I have given birth years when I knew them. Any assistance you can provide will be deeply appreciated.

From Gesaria (Kayseri), Ankara Vilayet:

Anahid Karamanian Stepanian, October 16, 1878 (mother)
Shoushan Stepanian Tsulikian, December 8, 1898 (sister)
Ovsanna Stepanian, July 23, 1904 (sister)
Tsangali Stepanian, June 1, 1907 (sister)
Dalita Stepanian, May 26, 1910 (sister)
Zarmineh Stepanian, 1851 (grandmother)

Hagop Stepanian 1867 (uncle), his wife Hasmig, and their sons Krikor 1896, Garabed 1897, Bedros 1899, and Boghos 1903

Sarkis Stepanian, 1869 (uncle), his wife Dzaghid, and their daughters Alvart 1905 and Marta 1907

Armen Stepanian, 1870 (uncle) and his wife Dikranouhi

Jivan Stepanian 1878 (uncle) and his wife Azniv 1884, their sons Hrahad 1904 and Kapriel 1905 and their daughter Narineh 1908

Levon Tsulikian 1891 (brother-in-law), his sister Markrid 1893 and their aunt Lousaper

My mother's family in Saraycik, also in Ankara Vilayet:

Khoren Karamanian, 1849 (grandfather)

Bedros Karamanian 1870 (uncle), his wife Lusine, and their sons Khoren, Taniel, Levon, Nazar, Thomas and Aram 1898 and their wives Mariam, Serine, Arpi, Datevig and Gadarine.

Kerop Karamanian (uncle), his wife Yevkeneh, their sons Sarkis, Vartan, Onnig and daughters Armine and Manishag

From Zmurnia (also known as Smyrna or Izmir):

Araxie Boghosian (née Bedrosian) my husband's aunt, her husband Dikran, and their children, Siroun 1895, Anoush 1896, and Apkar 1898

Please help me find my family. May God bless you for all the good work you are doing to assist our people.

Yours truly,
Khatoun Bedrosian
(née Stepanian)

GLOSSARY/NOTES — MAPS OF EUROPE

American Collegiate Institute	Secondary schools or colleges in Turkey were often run by American missionaries, hence the name
Asansör	elevator
bedel	sum paid for exemption from military service
belotte	French card game
duduk	Armenian wind instrument
Gesaria	Armenian name for Kayseri, a city in Central Anatolia
gradaran	reading room
harss	bride
lavash	bread
mistral	strong wind that blows through the south of France
Mount Argeus	Armenian name for Mount Erciyes
panir	cheese
raki	anise-flavoured hard liquor
sarma	stuffed grape leaves
Surb	Saint
Zmurnia	Armenian name for the ancient city of Smyrna now known as Izmir

THE VIEW FROM THE BLUFF

We've walked the straight path, you and I,
We have not cheated, compromised
Or lived the very slightest lie.
So let's march on, dear fate of mine!
My humble, truthful, faithful friend!
Keep marching on: there glory lies;
March forward — that's my testament.

TARAS SHEVCHENKO
FATE

I was born during the harvest, under a large oak at the edge of our family's best field. The sun was high in the sky, the air still and hot. Cicadas were thrumming all around us.

My body was small. Delicate. Unmistakably female.

Mama peered closer, afraid I was a trick of the light, a fancy of her imagination, but I proved real enough. After six sons, two of whom were married and with sons of their own, she had finally been blessed with a girl child.

A girl child.

She felt the shape and weight of the words on her tongue. Words she wanted to shout across the field, toss up to the sky, but couldn't. Even whispering them could be calamitous. So she sat back on her heels. Crossed herself three times. Thanked God for His gift, the Diva Mariya for her intercession, her long-dead mother for keeping her promise.

Mama wiped my face and body with the only *rushnyk* she had, still damp from the bread she had wrapped it around that morning, and wound me in her shawl. She smeared a little black earth on my forehead. Brushed my lips with a crust of bread. Placed me in the basket with the remnants of the kovbasa and goat cheese.

I like to think my first glimpse of the world was framed by the embroidery on the tablecloth she draped over the handle, that the air I first breathed was sharp with wheat.

Mama did not look in the basket again. After a brief rest, she returned to the section of the field where my father and brothers were working. Wading through the stalks of wheat, the joy flowing through her, seeping out of her pores like sweat, only sweeter smelling. Just another mouth to feed, she muttered under her breath, another crying baby to disturb our sleep. I don't care if she lives or dies, she declared, louder this time. How else could she protect me from evil spirits when her joy was drawing them out of every tree, field, and ravine? When fearlessness only invited calamity?

My father and brothers sang as they worked. Mama joined in, her voice strengthening with each step. *The stalks of wheat shiver, as far as the eye can see. While the sickle whispers: yield to me, yield to me...*

She placed the basket behind the last stook and started to rake, planting her feet wide apart to steady herself. She chased Mitya away when he lifted the tablecloth to look at me. Since no one else came near the basket or asked about the birth, she was able to hoard our surprise a while longer.

My mother thought everything about my birth was propitious – the rich dark soil beneath us, the stand of ancient oaks, the stalks of ripened wheat. Even the noise from the cicadas. My grandmother thought it was a disgrace.

"Does Osip not have enough sons to bring in the harvest," Baba complained as everyone returned from the fields, "without Olena having to give birth outside like a poor peasant's wife?"

Baba reached for the basket. Mama veered away, pushed past my father and brothers, and strode across the courtyard. She locked herself in her treatment room and when she stayed there for two days, the family thought there was something wrong with me, that I bore the marks of a child born late in a mother's life. Except for Mitya who had already figured out I was a girl. Not just any girl, but the first in three generations of Stetsenkos.

The village priest delayed my baptism for a few days to attend to his own field. So when my godparents brought me back from church and Baba asked them what name the priest had bestowed on her latest grandson, she was astonished to hear it was Nastasiya.

"Why didn't you tell me it was a girl?" she screamed at Mama, in front of our guests.

Mama offered no explanation. She wanted to savour the name while it was still fresh.

Nastasiya was her beloved mother's name, which Father Stepan could not have known as she came from another village, a two-day ride away. It was one more omen. As if my birth had not been omen enough.

My father didn't say a word. Not to Mama who had kept such a secret from him. Not to Baba who was berating him on his choice of a wife.

So here I am, the bit of yellow thread above the rim of the basket.

I've embroidered Mama raking, my father and brothers wielding their sickles, Oksana and Daryna tying and stacking the sheaves.

I've edged the cloth with oak leaves but I should have embroidered stalks of wheat, for wheat is more important than anything, I know that now, a truth as bitter as the bark of the oak tree.

Mama was a restless creature. She was happiest outside, working in the garden, taking care of the animals. Traipsing through the woods and meadows to collect the plants for her remedies. In winter, when the deep snows curtailed her wanderings, she retreated into herself, became listless and silent, like a songbird in a cage.

Every spring, once enough snow had melted but before the earth dissolved into mud, she would venture out of the village and walk for hours. Villagers reported their first sighting of Olena Mykolivna as a sure sign of spring. I became part of that ritual when Mama strapped me to her back with a shawl when I was eight months old.

"You look like a hunchback," Baba complained, "a peddler with a sack of wares."

Mama paid her no heed. My birth had shifted the dynamic between them.

What was it like to feel the sun and the wind on my cheeks for the first time in months? To sway as Mama scrambled over the uneven terrain, my head hovering above her shoulder, my eyes wide with all I could see of the world? Which *vesnianka* was she singing? There are so many songs about spring. She must've had a favourite.

This is Mama carrying me on her back. I've embroidered our eyes with the same blue thread, even though hers were brown, and I've extended the resemblance to the contour of our faces, the shape of our noses, a likeness in thread that we never shared in the flesh.

I've embroidered a grin on my fat little face and a kerchief over my curls to match the one on Mama's head.

I didn't inherit my mother's restless nature. I was happiest at home, with Baba, my cousin Lesya, my brothers' wives and their children.

What I loved most was to watch my sisters-in-law embroider, their needles darting in and out of the cloth like dragonflies. Baba could no longer embroider, she was almost blind, but she ran her hands over each newly-finished piece, bringing the linen up to her nose as if she could smell the colours, the intricacies of the pattern. She had a large trunk filled with clothes and linens her mother, grandmother and great-grandmother had embroidered, some of them more than a hundred years old. She would often pull out a shawl, a blouse, or a rushnyk and ask me to describe it so she could tell me the story behind it.

If Mama was in hearing distance, she would call me to the kitchen or send me to fetch something from her treatment room. Her lack of embroidery skills had ruined her relationship with Baba from the beginning and she didn't want my head filled with nonsense about the sacredness of needlework.

That winter day, I was sitting on a stool beside Lesya, hoop in hand, pulling a needle in and out of the linen. Oksana and Daryna were busy with their own needlework and Baba was sleeping through the noise Yakiv and Pavlo were making as they chased each other around her chair. Mama was cutting vegetables for the noon meal. Not that I remember anything about that day, I was only three.

"What have you embroidered for me today?" Lesya asked as she rolled up her own needlework in a white cloth on her lap. She was Mama's niece and had lived with us since I was a baby.

"A *kvitka*," I answered, handing her my hoop.

Lesya expected to see a cluster of random stitches, not a perfectly formed blue flower. "Where did you get this?"

"I made it."

"You couldn't have embroidered this, my dove. Now tell me before your grandmother finds out you've been cutting up her *rushnyky*."

"I saw the flower. In my head. The needle knew the way."

When Lesya showed my mother the flower I had embroidered, Mama crossed herself and pressed the linen to her chest. It reminded her of a flower that grew by the river near her village and that she had never been able to find here.

Oksana and Daryna rushed over to see what I had done. Held the scrap of linen up to the light of the window, marvelling at the intricacy of the pattern, the neatness of my stitching. Mama soon tired of the fuss and returned to her vegetables. My sisters-in-law to their handwork.

Baba was awake now so I showed her the flower I had embroidered. Although Baba later claimed she had enough vision in her left eye to see the flower and appreciate how finely it was wrought, Lesya remembered it differently. Recounted how Baba had traced the flower with her finger, over and over, tears in her rheumy eyes.

The flower I'd embroidered didn't figure on any of the linens Baba had inherited from her family, the few pieces my mother had brought from her home village, or the ones Oksana and Daryna had prepared for their wedding chests. When Father Stepan claimed he'd seen one like it on an altar cloth in Poltava where he was first ordained as a priest, the women laughed at him as men could not be relied upon to remember such things.

"Are you sure you didn't embroider that flower yourself and forget about it?" I asked Lesya whenever she told me the story.

"How could I forget such a flower," she invariably replied, "when I have never seen its likeness in thread or in nature? When it could only be the work of an *ànhel*?"

The next time I sat down with my embroidery, there was no guidance from the needle, no flower waiting to be stitched. Weeks, months passed without the miracle repeating itself. I had to learn to embroider like everyone else. Mama was relieved but Baba kept the scrap of linen with the blue flower in her trunk, convinced that I had inherited her gift with the needle, that I would one day be the caretaker of her family's heirlooms.

I've embroidered an *ànhel* on the stool beside Lesya, pulling a needle out of the linen. Mama cutting vegetables in the kitchen.

Baba asleep in her chair, the boys chasing each other around her. Oksana and Daryna huddled over their embroidery frames.

I'm playing with Marusiya. I was not the only girl for long, you see. My sisters-in-law had four girls, one after another. Marusiya, Katya, Anoushka, and Svitlana.

It was as if my birth had removed a family curse.

The villagers appreciated Mama even if Baba did not. She was their *znakharka* and they relied on her hands to diagnose their ills and her knowledge of plants to cure them. She had such a magical touch with animals they also called on her when theirs were in distress.

The old znakharka was still alive when my mother arrived in the village as Osip's bride but by the time she died three years later, so many had sampled Mama's teas, poultices, and remedies that a line formed outside our door before the old woman was in her grave.

It didn't take long for the villagers to realize that Mama had a greater gift, for her reputation to spread far and wide. People gathered at our door in such numbers that Tato had to convert one of the stables into a treatment room. If Mama's inability to embroider was Baba's first disappointment in her son's choice of a wife, her gift for healing was the second.

I always accompanied my mother on her foraging expeditions, small basket in hand. We gathered herbs, berries, grasses, mushrooms and flowers. She taught me the names of the plants, how to collect them, how to wrap their roots in wet rags. Explained which plant or part of the plant cured which ailment long before I could understand what she was teaching me. Mama was determined to pass on her own mother's knowledge and skills, even though my brother Mitya was the worthier candidate.

Birds perched on Mama's shoulders and the creatures of the forest gathered around us as we worked. I never lost my fear of them, especially the foxes, who stared at me the same way they stared at our chickens.

Baba scolded Mama if I returned from such an expedition with cuts or scratches on my hands. She didn't want me to tie the sheaves at harvest time or thresh the grain or take on any chore that might roughen my hands but Mama insisted I participate. "You were born outside, at harvest time," she liked to remind me, "surrounded by the wheat that will feed you and your children and your children's children. Fancy embroidery won't fill their empty bellies."

When I was six, Baba arranged for Lesya and I to take lessons from Ahnesa Andriyivna, the priest's wife, and the best needlewoman in our village. She had included Lesya to blunt my mother's objections, knowing how fond Mama was of her niece.

Mama objected to the arrangement anyway. She didn't want me around the priest or his wife, afraid they would lure me away as they had Mitya. Lending him books, teaching him to draw, getting him to gather specimens for their experiments.

Ahnesa Andriyivna was unlike any woman in the village. She was elegant, slight of build and as pale as bleached linen. Her large, haunting eyes were amber, the same colour as the stones at the bottom of our creek. People called her *malo solovey*, little nightingale, because of her clear, bright voice. Crowded into our church to hear her sing.

The house she shared with Father Stepan had the same thatched roof, whitewashed walls, and clay floor as the other houses in the village but once you crossed its threshold, you stepped into another world. A world of books and icons, rocks and plant specimens, small dead animals in jars, insects pinned to linen, beautiful ones like butterflies and dragonflies and fat ugly ones that you couldn't bear to look at. There was an unfinished banner on a large embroidery frame, works at different stages of completion on two smaller frames and pieces awaiting a final touch in hoops scattered here and there. There were icons everywhere – Father Stepan was an icon painter – but also drawings of animals and plants, on the walls and in sketchbooks stacked on a large side table.

My first lesson was a disappointment. Ahnesa Andriyivna never looked at the samples of needlework I had brought nor did she ask me what stitches I knew. She gave me a needle and asked me to hold it, firmly but not too tightly, to roll it between my fingers, to press it into my skin. As if I'd never held a needle in my life, as if I'd never embroidered that blue flower.

When she showed me how to divide the thread and explained which end to slip through the eye of the needle, I blinked back tears. I already knew how to separate strands of thread. I was always doing it for Oksana and Daryna because my fingers were smaller than theirs and I had more patience. Was I not to learn anything new?

I glanced at Lesya but she didn't lift her eyes from the stitches Ahnesa Andriyivna had asked her to practise, stitches even I knew. The priest's wife spent the rest of the lesson on the correct way to hold the needle and to push it through the fabric depending on the type of stitch.

Before we left, she gave us each a packet of needles from England. We couldn't believe it.

When Baba asked me what I had learned in my first lesson, I placed the needle packet in her hand to distract her. She felt the edges of it with her fingers, counted the number of needles, surprised by such a generous gift.

"They come from England," I told her, a country that Mitka had often mentioned. He was planning to go there, to board a ship for Canada, but none of us knew that yet.

"Choose one needle and put away the packet. Keep the needle hidden when you are not using it and never lend it to anyone. It absorbs your energy and transmits it to everything you embroider."

When I showed the packet to Mitya later, he immediately took out the little sketch pad the priest had given him and drew the elephant on the wrapping.

"Are there elephants in England?"

He laughed and shook his head. "But there are elephants in India and Africa and the British think they own the world. Which might account for them putting elephants on their needle packets."

That was the way Mitya answered questions. With a possibility instead of a definitive statement. Ahnesa Andriyivna also spoke in possibilities. "The hole in the needle is called an eye for a reason," she told me that first day, "so the needle can see where it's going, even if you can't." Was she referring to the embroidering incident when I was three, when I told Lesya the needle knew the way?

The priest and his wife encouraged us to explore their home, examine their specimens, leaf through their albums. We soon understood why Mitya spent so much time at their house. There were so many treasures, we didn't know where to look. I always saved enough time to linger over the processional banner. There were stools around the frame as several women in the village were helping Ahnesa Andriyivna with it and I would move from one to the other, admiring the stitches that had been added since I last looked at it. A similar banner, of Our Lord Jesus Christ, already hung in our church but I thought this one, of Our Holy Mother of God, was more beautiful, especially the face. It was Father Stepan who had drawn the Diva Mariya on the silk and despite his best intentions, he had drawn the face, the eyes of his wife.

Here is the large frame that holds the processional banner and the women who worked on it: Ahnesa Andriyivna, Galina Mykolivna, Oleksandra Pavlivna, and Nadya Petrivna.

I've embroidered them all on one side so you can admire the beautiful face, the large haunting eyes of the Diva Mariya.

Since Mama spent so much time gathering plants, Baba prevailed on her to dye our embroidery thread. At first she did not deviate from the colours commonly used in the embroidery of our village. She crushed sunflower seed husks for black, acorns for blue-grey hues, birch leaves for yellow, and oak bark for orange.

But she was soon experimenting with other ingredients, especially for the yellows and blues, to add to their range. From the pale yellow of a baby's hair to the deep yellow of a sunflower petal. From the fragile blue of a lark's egg to the greenish blue of a summer sky before a storm.

When she dragged the dyeing vats into the yard every fall, after the harvest and the ploughing had been done, our neighbours would gather, their arms full of homespun floss, and she would let them soak their thread with ours. Much to Baba's chagrin as she would have preferred the colours for our exclusive use.

I remember the skeins of thread hanging to dry between the trees, like a rainbow that had unravelled.

Mitya. I've embroidered my brother from the back because he was always on his way somewhere. Because he was a *mandrivnyk*, a wanderer.

He first wandered away at the age of three, all the way to the next village. He was never a climber. Fences and trees didn't interest him. It was distance he craved.

He would disappear for hours, for days at a time in the summer, except during harvest. He loved books but hated the classroom. Couldn't stand being inside. It was Father Stepan who recognized Mitya's intelligence and the restlessness that plagued him, who devised ways for Mitya to learn outside. Who taught him how to draw everything he came across: trees, leaves, flowers, animals, birds, and insects. How to gather specimens and identify them in *The Compendium of the Natural World*.

I've embroidered Mitya at the edge of the woods. With a small rucksack on his back, a walking stick in his hand, and a cap on his unruly hair. He's fourteen, a boy-man. The last summer he was home. Before he entered the seminary in Poltava, the seminary Father Stepan knew would never be able to hold him.

Sometimes when I push the needle through the cloth, I hear a tiny puff of air, like the softest of sighs. It was Ahnesa Andriyivna who taught me to listen for it, to notice everything when I'm embroidering, from the needle piercing the fabric, the thread tickling my palm, to the slight creak of the frame. When I separate strands of thread, my finger running down between them, I can sometimes smell the colour. Like Baba did. A trace of acorn or birch leaf lingering in the thread, aching to be released.

Tato. I've embroidered my father standing in a field with his sickle, the wheat waist high, the sky a delicate blue. He is like that oak tree I was born under, strong, tall and very large.

He was a quiet man but his voice was so deep, it startled people, especially those who'd been lulled by his silence. When Mama disagreed with Baba, he never took her side and if my brothers argued, he didn't intervene either, letting Foma settle the matter, while Mama glared at him for not keeping the boys in line.

Marusiya was fifteen months younger than I and we were inseparable, closer than sisters. She was my brother Foma's child but I never thought of her as my niece.

We were always hiding. In the apple and cherry trees that bordered the garden, in the barn, the stables, the root cellar, and in the large chests that lined Mama's treatment room. Marusiya was daring in her choice of hiding places and sometimes had to be rescued.

Like the time she decided to climb the ancient oak, the one I was born under. It was during harvest and everyone was resting after the noon meal. She urged me to climb it with her but I didn't want to get into trouble.

When it was time to resume work, Marusiya was still in the tree. Her father went searching for her, ringing the bell so she could find her way through the stalks that were as tall as she was.

I was too afraid of Foma to tell him where Marusiya was but Oksana noticed that my eyes kept straying to the tree.

"Marusiya, come down this instant," she called up once Foma was out of earshot. There was no reply.

"You will have to fetch her for me."

I was reluctant but allowed her to boost me to the first branch. I didn't like climbing, only ever did it to please Marusiya, and the oak was more forbidding than the trees we usually climbed together. The bark was cutting into my hands and knees and snagging my clothes, which made progress difficult.

"You have to come down," I called up, when I finally saw the edge of her skirt in the darkness. "Before your father comes back."

"I can't move, Stasiya. I'm too scared."

All the hours I'd spent under that tree hadn't prepared me for the dark green space I was moving through. Light and noise barely penetrated the thick canopy. I could see why spirits would want to live there. Who could resist such a private place?

What would it be like to sit here in the middle of the night with only an owl's eyes for company?

I kept going, afraid to look down, to freeze like Marusiya had done.

Singing softly, to calm her.

Marusiya.

Her eyes were so big and round and blue, you could remember nothing else about her face. I've embroidered the edge of her page with cornflowers, with the thread that Mama once dyed to match her granddaughter's eyes.

She is perched on one of the outer branches of the oak tree, the dark green foliage like a halo around her. Her hair is falling out of her braid, her kerchief askew, her bare feet showing beneath her linen skirt.

She's not clinging to the branch or showing any fear but sitting straight and strong, her eyes on the horizon, on the road that leads to the next village. For Marusiya had a touch of Mama's restlessness, of Mitya's wandering ways.

When Uncle Borys died without wife or child, Foma decided to move his family into the dead man's house. Oksana didn't want to part from Daryna, Yakiv from Pavlo, and Marusiya from me but Foma ignored us all. We wailed for weeks, even little Svitlana, who didn't understand what was happening.

Mitya left the seminary in Poltava and wandered farther west. To Galicia, to Germany, to England. In Liverpool, he boarded a ship to Canada.

Lesya returned to her village to marry.

Bohdan took over his father-in-law's blacksmith shop and house which meant that Daryna and Pavlo, Katya and Anoushka, also moved out.

And so even when you live in a village where nothing ever changes, your life does.

When Ahnesa Andriyivna arranged for me to study church embroidery in Poltava, at the convent where she herself had trained, Maman refused to let me go. She was still angry at the priest and his wife for setting Mitya on the path that had taken him away from us.

There could be no higher calling than embroidering for the Church and the greater glory of God, Baba insisted. Healing was also a higher calling, Mama countered, although she knew I did not have a talent for it. Mama and Baba argued about it for weeks until Oksana intervened by writing to her sister who lived in Poltava. Ohla Sergeyivna offered to visit me at the convent every week and report back to the family. Mama, who was fond of Oksana and her sister, conceded.

No one asked me if I wanted to go, if I was ready to leave my family, my village.

The journey to Poltava etched a path in my mind as relentlessly as the waters of the Vorskla River carved the valley we travelled through. A path that has changed the way I view my life and the way I will leave it.

Uncle Hryhoriy took me there in his wagon in May of 1914. I didn't know this uncle since he had gone to work for the railroad at a young age and had only recently returned. He kept to himself, in a cabin he built at the edge of the woods, so I was surprised when he turned out to be talkative. Maybe he needed the motion of the wagon to loosen his tongue. Maybe, after all those years of working on trains, he needed the world to be blurring by, not that our wagon moved fast enough to blur anything.

"I worked the Kyiv-Moskva line most of my life but I did spend some time on the Great Siberian Way. When it was first built and most of the bridges were temporary and there were very few stations and we didn't know when we went into a tunnel whether we would be coming out the other end."

"And what was Siberia like, Uncle?"

"Empty. Cold. Beautiful."

He stopped after each word as if only sentences could do them justice.

"Godforsaken."

Godforsaken. A word Mitya might fancy, as it was both sacred and bleak.

I didn't want to think about Mitya, forever lost to us. I had just left Mama and Marusiya. My Baba. Tato. The boys. Oksana and Daryna. Katya, Anoushka and Svitlana. So I tried to imagine the Siberian landscape my uncle had admired from the train. In all its cold and empty beauty, in all its Godforsakeness.

I had never been anywhere. I only knew our village, our fields, our woods. The steppe and the sky above it.

As the wagon wobbled over the road, my eyes flitted from tree to tree, from field to sky, eager for the landscape to change. But we only encountered more fields, more woods, more villages. Even the people we met seemed familiar.

When Mitya first wrote to us from Manitoba and described the prairie stretching out under a wide expanse of blue, just like our steppe, we wondered why he'd travelled so far to settle in a place just like home.

The landscape started to change when we reached the Vorskla River.

"Some people claim that Vorskla means thief of glass in Old Russian," my uncle told me, after we had travelled along its bank for a few *versts*.

Thief of glass. Mitya would like that too.

"...but it just means swampy river. And as you can see, more swamp than river."

I had never seen a river or a swamp, only the creek near our village. What surprised me was the movement, the way the river flowed away from us, steadily, determinedly, expecting us to follow, unlike the road which depended on us to move over it. I loved the way the water carried everything with her: the sky, the clouds, the willows, our silhouettes on the road.

"The Dnipro, now there's a river. The Volga. The Lena."

Mama was born in a village on the Dnipro, not far from Kremenchug, a two-day journey from our home. Maybe it was growing up near a river that had made her so restless. The flow of the water pulling at the blood in her veins like the moon tugs at the sea.

The river had widened a little and we had left the marshier sections behind when it happened. When I crossed some invisible boundary and fell into the landscape.

Clouds filled the wagon.

Wheat sprouted in the middle of the road, the shoots a delicate green.

The river flowed through my veins.

I could smell everything. The wormwood that grew on the sides of the road, dead animals I couldn't see, the mud at the bottom of the river. Hear everything. The pebbles scattering under the wheels of the wagon, the bit clanging against the horse's teeth, the coins shifting in Uncle Hryhoriy's pocket.

Most Glorious Ever-Virgin Mary, Mother of Christ our God, receive my humble prayer. I tried to summon the Diva Mariya's lovely face from Ahnesa Andriyivna's banner but I couldn't hold it in my mind or the prayer to my lips.

Had Mitya been transformed by his long journey? Had the swell of the ocean, the vastness of the Canadian prairie forever altered the boy we once knew?

This is me in the wagon with Uncle Hryhoriy. Wearing the clothes Baba had chosen for my journey, each garment embroidered by a different generation.

The *hustka* is the oldest, the handiwork of Baba's great-grandmother. I remember that shawl, the weight of its years on my shoulders.

I've embroidered the river, the willows leaning into it, the first houses of a village in the distance, the wormwood at the edge of the road.

My uncle is looking straight ahead but my head is turned, my eyes are on the river.

I arrived at the convent late at night, a blur of dark buildings and street lights my only glimpse of Poltava. When I woke up the next morning in the dormitory, I was surrounded by noisy girls asking questions. What's your name? Where are you from? Why are you wearing those ridiculous clothes?

Sister Yulia's clubfoot banging on the stairs sent them scurrying to the chests at the end of their beds from which they pulled out black frocks.

There was a similar frock at the end of my bed and I hastily drew it over my head. It was so big on me the other girls laughed. As I lined up to wash my face, I crossed the two funnels of sunlight that met in the middle of the floor, coming from the small windows set high in the stone walls on either side. The convent had many such funnels, I was to discover, as most of its windows were high-set. I had expected austerity but not a rationing of light.

I was taken to Sister Lyudmyla after breakfast. A tall woman with a stoop, a sharp nose, and feet so big her shoes stuck out from beneath her habit. The room we were in was long and narrow, overlooking a courtyard, two embroidery frames at each window. So I was to have daylight after all and for this I was grateful.

"Ahnesa Andriyivna claims you see patterns in your head which you have never been taught."

"Yes, Sister."

"Here is a piece of linen and some thread. I want you to embroider something for me. From your imagination."

How could I tell her that I didn't imagine the patterns, that they came to me, fully formed, like visions? Like memories of another life?

After I stretched the linen on the frame, I slipped the blue thread, pale and unpretentious, through the needle's eye. The novice sitting across from me was working with purple silk and gold metallic thread. Embroidering a cross of Saint Ohla.

I waited, needle poised, having never summoned a pattern before. I could recall any pattern I learned, no matter how complex, but not the ones that appeared to me. Those often faded away before I could figure them out, before I could commit them to cloth.

The young woman looked up from her Saint Ohla's cross to smile at me.

And then I saw it, a whorl of blue thread, twisted and doubled back, like the edge of a petal. Another whorl. The whole flower. Linked to another and another, on the upper part of a sleeve. Now I could see the whole dress, the woman wearing it. Her sad, weary face.

"Are you unwell?" The young woman was now standing beside me. "You cried out. Shall I fetch Sister Lyudmyla?"

"No. I– I must've had a spell."

The flower was still in my mind's eye so I worked quickly to capture it before it disappeared.

When Sister Lyudmyla returned, she removed the linen from the frame. Held it up to the light of the window. Examined both sides. I didn't tell her about the woman. The dress. Didn't tell her the flower was the one I had inexplicably embroidered when I was three.

I liked the smells of the convent: the wax the nuns put on their floors which were made of wood, the candles and the incense they burned in the chapel. The sweetness of so many girls after the stale and sour smell of my father and brothers.

We couldn't see the street but we could hear the noise of the city as it pressed against the walls that surrounded the convent's gardens. Vendors hawking their wares, children playing, wagons rolling over cobblestones.

We weren't allowed to leave the convent. Ahnesa Andriyivna had warned me about that but I figured it wouldn't bother me. How was I to know I would feel trapped? That I would miss the steppe, the vastness of the sky, the hours I used to spend outside, almost as much as I would miss my family?

Oksana's sister came to visit me every Sunday. Ohla Sergeyivna was more vivacious than Oksana and more worldly than Ahnesa Andriyivna. She had been sent to Poltava to attend the gymnasium, to escape the fate of her sisters. She had married a wealthy merchant, a widower with many sons. She was so fascinating I looked forward to her visits. She always brought me something, a book, candy, or little cakes which made me popular with the other girls.

War broke out.

I had to return to my village.

Four of my brothers were conscripted into the Imperial Army. Vanya was the only one spared to work the farm with my father. I was grateful that Mitya was so far away, safe in his house on the Manitoba prairie.

Oksana and Daryna and their children moved back into the house.

Foma died within days of reaching the front and Bohdan lasted a year before he returned to us, maimed and no longer in his right mind.

Kostya and Yaroslav came home after the revolution pulled Russia out of the war. Thin in their tattered uniforms. Their faces burnt by the sun. Their eyes flinty and cold.

Here is Baba lying on the bench, under the watchful eyes of the icons Father Stepan had painted for us. She is dressed in the shirt, vest, and skirt she wore when she married my grandfather.

I've reproduced the whitework on the sleeves and edge of her *vyshiv-anka*, the leaf and blossom patterns on her vest. She is holding a cross in her hands.

Tato and his brothers, Hryhoriy, Iwan, and Timofei, are sitting beside the body. I am huddling in the corner with Marusiya, Katya, Anoushka and Svitlana.

Outside the window, I've embroidered the owl that heralded her death. We both heard it but I was so busy trying to catch a glimpse of it in the darkness I failed to notice its effect on Baba. When she bade me goodbye instead of good night, feeling my face with her hands, I thought she was confused. The next morning she was dead.

I returned to Poltava with Marusiya in the fall of 1918. She was to attend the same gymnasium as her aunt and I was to resume my training at the convent, while we both boarded at her aunt's house. Ahnesa Andriyivna was surprised that Sister Lyudmyla had agreed to this arrangement.

The convent was not far from the house but I didn't always go there directly. I often walked down Dvoryanska Street, past the music school and the military hospital, turning on to Frunze with its lovely houses, and then Olexandrivksa Street with its many shops. But if there were German soldiers on Dvoryanska, I would take a shorter, less interesting route.

Sister Lyudmyla was kinder to me than she had been four years earlier. She didn't praise my work but entrusted me with beautiful silks and linens, threads of silver and gold.

I spent long hours at the convent. My eyes smarted, my fingers throbbed, but the light was as soft as the silk under my fingers, the silence as deep as the well in the garden. It was a respite from the tumult of Ohla Sergeyivna's house, the intense discussions around the table. About politics, Ukrainian independence, the German occupation.

One morning when I rang the bell, Sister Yulia didn't come to the door. I waited and rang the bell again.

"The good sisters are gone," a passer-by told me. "They left early this morning."

I returned home, dejected, but Ohla Sergeyivna already knew someone who could continue my apprenticeship, who had taught at the embroidery workshop in Reshetylivska.

Anna Dimitrivna dressed like a man, smoked cigarettes, and drank too much vodka. She was still in bed when I arrived at her flat for my lesson every afternoon. The embroidery she taught me was not liturgical but just as rich and ornamental. Adorning evening dresses instead of priestly vestments, linens for banquet tables instead of altars. She had, however, nothing but contempt for her clients, for their beautiful dresses and linens. Anna Dimitrivna was a passionate socialist, one of the many debaters who gathered at the home of Ohla Sergeyivna and her husband, Mykhailo Petrovych, who were both committed to an independent Ukraine.

I found the discussions around the table bewildering. Were the Germans protecting our fledgling independence or were they only after our wheat? Were the Bolsheviks going to liberate us or enslave us?

What would happen after the Germans left? Once the Bolsheviks arrived?

There was talk of counter-revolution.

Foreign interference.

Civil war.

The Rotunda was my favourite place in Poltava. It was not far from the house and although Ohla Sergeyivna had forbidden Marusiya and me to venture there on our own, her stepsons were only too glad to escort us.

I loved to stand on the bluff and look down at the valley, at the river dragging its blue light thorough the fields and woods and villages. You could see so far in every direction. You could imagine the world.

It was there that I met Yuriy one afternoon. Marusiya had wandered away with her cousins and I was reading a book of poetry her uncle had lent me. I had never read poetry in Ukrainian before, only in Russian.

A young man sat down on the opposite bench. I recognized him. He was a close friend of Ohla Sergeyivna's stepson Petro, not that I could remember his name or patronymic.

When he rose again and bridged the short distance between us, I didn't know where to look so I stared at his boots.

"Yuriy Oleksandrovych," he kindly reintroduced himself. "A pleasure to meet you again, Nastasiya Osipinova."

"The pleasure is mine, Yuriy Oleksandrovych."

He was still holding my hand. When the book started to slip from my lap, he caught it before it fell to the ground.

"Ah, the poems of Lesya Ukrainka. What any Ukrainian girl should be reading while German soldiers walk the streets of Poltava and the Bolsheviks wait at the gates."

I didn't know if he was mocking me.

Marusiya was standing at the parapet, too far to be of any help. She knew how to talk to strangers. I didn't.

"Will you walk with me?"

I scrambled to my feet and almost stepped on his.

He smiled and proffered his arm. I placed my hand on his coat sleeve, my fingers skidding on the black wool. I was back in

Uncle Hryhoriy's wagon, crossing an invisible boundary, falling into another landscape.

I went to the cinema on Olexandrivksa Street with Marusiya, her cousins and their friends, to see my first film, *The Queen of Spades*. I knew the story – I had read it at school – but nothing prepared me for actors moving across a brightly lit screen. It was all so intimate, as if we were in their drawing room, peering over their shoulders as they played cards.

The second time I went to see the film, Yuriy Oleksandrovych was sitting beside me and I couldn't concentrate. I was listening to him breathe, laugh, whisper to his friends. Smelling the damp wool of his coat, the polish on his boots.

Yuriy wrote poetry but was studying at the Teacher Training Institute. He was too poor to accompany Petro and his brothers on their social rounds but Ohla Sergeyivna often invited him to dinner, to ensure he ate properly several times a week.

After the film, we returned to the house. There were still people around the table, in full discussion.

"You don't like politics, Nastasiya Osipinova?" Yuriy asked as he steered me to the drawing room where other, less vehement debates were underway.

"I have nothing but a village education, Yuriy Alexandrovich. I'm afraid I have little to contribute."

"You've read Lesya Ukrainka's poetry. It's very political."

"Poetry lends itself to musings about politics, Yuriy Oleksandrovych," I replied, "life and death." I did not say *love* but found myself blushing anyway. "I only know embroidery. My needle cannot save the world or feed a hungry child."

"But embroidery is an art, is it not? Shevchenko wrote about embroidering a book while he was in captivity, about embroidering his grief."

"He was just being fanciful. I'm sure he never threaded a needle in his life!"

Yuriy laughed, his eyes holding mine. Eyes like Ahnesa Andriyivna's, reminding me not only of the stones at the bottom of our creek but the water running over them, shot through with light.

Weeks passed.

The discussions around the table were more and more disturbing.

Ohla Sergeyivna wanted to send us back to our village.

Anna Dimitrivna was distracted, impatient. I was learning nothing.

It was morning and the river was still, like a sheet of glass, stolen or not. Mirroring the sky, the clouds, the willows with their flimsy branches and yellow leaves. Marusiya was talking to me but I was listening to Yuriy's voice behind us, deep in conversation with Petro and his brothers. They were talking about going to Kyiv, about making a stand there.

A stand. It was always about making a stand. Not what came after. The falling down. The lying dead in the street.

"Aunt Ohla says everything will escalate once the Germans leave..."

Hadn't there been enough killing? Were Yakiv and Pavlo to be sacrificed now? Petro and his brothers? And Yuriy, my beloved Yuriy?

Everything that had been discussed at the Martenkos came to pass.

The Germans pulled out.

The Bolsheviks came.

Symon Petliura and his volunteers drove the Bolsheviks out but they came back again. Then it was the White Army's turn.

And that was only in the first six months.

Mykhailo Petrovych was arrested as were three of his sons. Yuriy and Petro escaped just before the White Army arrived. Anna Dimitrivna, was killed as were several Jewish students who had frequented the Martenko home.

There was counter-revolution.

Foreign intervention.

Civil war.

Ukraine lost its independence.

There was cholera. Typhus. Famine.

When I returned to my village, I moved into Uncle Hryhoriy's cabin at the edge of the woods. He had written me a few letters over the years, fuelled by vodka from the sound of them, but I never thought he would leave me the cabin and a small pouch of gold coins.

The family farm was much diminished. Kostya and Yaroslav drank and gambled, paying little heed to Vanya, who had worked the farm in their absence and since their return. Oksana had remarried and Daryna had moved Bohdan and the last of their children to the house by the forge.

Mama ate and slept in her treatment room. Her healing practice was as busy as ever and I helped by gathering the plants she needed and preparing the more common remedies.

Tato was now totally silent. He looked after the animals and the garden, which had once been Mama's responsibilities. The rest of the time he wandered. Across the fields, through the woods, down the road to the next village. As if he were taking over from Mama there too.

I turned down two offers of marriage although I hadn't heard from Yuriy since he'd fled Poltava with Petro. I spent my evenings embroidering with Ahnesa Andriyivna and the other village women. We were working on a third processional banner, this one depicting the patron of our church, Saint Mykola.

As much as I loved being close to Mama, living in my cabin by the woods, I missed the bustle of the town, the liveliness of Ohla Sergeyivna's house. I missed Marusiya and her cousins and their friends. And Yuriy, my beloved Yuriy.

This is Uncle Hryhoriy's cabin. My cabin. The large garden in front, the woods behind. Newly dyed thread hangs on the clothesline. Dyeing thread is a difficult, tedious process. Colour is surprisingly elusive.

I've embroidered myself in the window, looking out.

I was on my knees in the garden when Yuriy came. He'd been travelling for days. From Krakow to Kyiv, Kyiv to Poltava, Poltava to the station closest to our village. His shadow fell across my vegetables and I didn't look up, thinking it was one of my brothers. Or Anton Bohdanovych, the more persistent of my suitors, hoping I had changed my mind.

"Are you not pleased to see me, Nastasiya Osipinova?"

The shadow was real but I thought my longing had conjured up his voice. When I checked the man's boots, I was reminded of another pair I had stared at once.

"Did you not receive my letters?"

I wiped my dirty hands on my apron and got off my knees. Shaded my eyes from the sun. Anxious now to confront the impostor, to chase him off my land.

But it was Yuriy. His face and clothes caked with dust.

We embraced. Formally. And then less so.

"I can only stay a few days," he said. "I must return to Poltava to finish my teacher training."

Here is Yuriy sitting under a tree outside my cabin, writing a poem. His hair is long and falling over his glasses, his collar. His clothes are shabby, his boots worn, but he cuts an elegant figure anyway.

I've embroidered myself under the same tree. Working on an altar cloth for the church in the next village.

I can't embroider the happiness that settled on us that day. Although his bag was already packed and he was leaving the next morning.

Yuriy wrote often but mail delivery was sporadic. I would go for weeks without a letter and then receive four. His letters were like his poems, like the prayers Father Stepan recited on feast days, like the *vesnianky* my mother sang to me as a child.

I half expected the pages to burst into life, to become birds and butterflies and angels, their wings fluttering in my face.

Who was I to fantasize about the fluttering of wings? To have poems written about me?

I had become someone else, a woman who made love to a man not her husband and didn't feel shame about it, a woman who read poetry and novels and political tracts, a woman who smoked a cigarette and drank a glass of *horilka* every evening as the sun went down.

By the time Yuriy finished his teacher training in Poltava, I had received the calf the church had promised me in exchange for the altar cloth I was working on when he came. I named her Krasulka, pretty one, and put her in the small shelter I had built for the pig and the goats. She howled all night and would not be consoled.

Yuriy was offered a teaching post in Kyiv. I would've followed him there but Mama needed me. Vanya was overworked, his wife unwell. Kostya and Yaroslav were abusive. Oksana had a new husband and mother-in-law. Daryna had her hands full with Bohdan who had never recovered from his war injuries. Who sat at the table, like an overgrown child, attending to whatever small task she gave him.

I decided to stay without discussing it with Mama. Which was not unusual. We only ever spoke of everyday things. The harvest, the weather, her plants, her animals. Although Oksana had read her the letters I had written from Poltava, she never asked me about my life there, the convent, Ohla Sergeyivna's house. When Yuriy left after his brief visit, she never asked about him either.

When she disappeared one day, we looked for her everywhere, thinking she had fallen or exhausted herself on one of her long rambles. We had the whole village combing the fields, woods, and ravines. After a week, I was the only one still looking for her, traipsing through the fields and woods she loved so much.

When I returned to the cabin one day, tired and discouraged, I found Baba's trunk on my hearth. Vanya's wife had it sent over, thinking it belonged to my mother. I pulled out the clothes and linens and spread them through the cabin, remembering the stories my Baba had told me about each piece. I hadn't been through her trunk since I'd taken out the bundle of clothes she had prepared for her funeral. It was only later, as I was falling asleep, that I realized that the few embroidered pieces my mother had brought from her village were missing. Baba used to keep them at the very bottom of her trunk as if they'd contaminate her family's heirlooms.

Mama wasn't dead. She had gone back to her village on the Dnipro River and taken those few pieces of embroidery with her – they were all she had of her mother and grandmother. Mama had returned to her village to live with Lesya and her family. Leaving me free to follow Yuriy to Kyiv.

I cried for days in my cabin by the woods.

I've embroidered Mama at the age of seven. Stepping into the Dnipro River by herself. The water is icy cold, the current strong.

The restlessness of the river seeps into her blood, her bones, a restlessness she'll pass on to Mitya and through Foma to Marusiya.

She told me once that she had fallen into the river at that age, that the current had swept her along, that an invisible hand had plucked her from the water and dropped her on the shore, wet and cold and breathless.

This is Mama gathering her beloved plants, which I've embroidered in all their feathery greenness.

There is a bird hovering over her shoulder, a fox watching from behind a tree.

I'm standing beside her, holding her large basket.

This is Mama on the road, walking away from us. She's carrying Mitya's rucksack on her back and swinging the walking stick he carved for her before he left for Poltava.

I've embroidered a winding road although the road leaving our village is straight. Roads are dangerous, Mama used to say. Once you set foot on one, there's no guarantee you'll return.

Standing on the bluff in Poltava prepared me for the grandeur of Kyiv. A city I fell in love with from the moment I stepped off the train. The buildings, the squares, the parks. The hills and the steep streets that wound around them. The trees everywhere. The Dnipro River.

There was so much noise. Movement. Wagons, carriages, tramcars, several automobiles. Even the people walked quickly.

If you looked closely, the city's grandeur was deceptive. Kyiv had changed hands more often than Poltava during the civil war. Sixteen times in eighteen months. Or some such number. There were bullet holes in the stones and bricks of the houses, on their shutters and roofs. Many shops were closed and those that were open had very little merchandise on display. There were beggars on the street. Children running wild. Whole families without shelter. They slept where they could. In the lobbies and stairwells of once grand buildings. In alleyways, huddling under empty rifle crates.

Yet there were people in the restaurants and cafés, musicians playing on street corners, people lining up to see films on Khrashchatyk Street. The cinemas had been nationalised, given new names, but everyone still called them the Crystal, the Metropol, the Chary.

I ignored the shabbiness. Concentrated on the buildings that were intact, the shops that were still open. The people on the sidewalks, on the trams, in the queues. The sky, the changing hues of the river, the way the fog gathered half way up the hills, the chestnut trees in full bloom, their white petals dropping on us as we strolled through the park.

There was more Russian spoken in Kyiv than in Poltava. Yuriy was incensed that he had to teach in Russian, that no progress had been made in introducing Ukrainian as the language of education. Yuriy had diverted the hopes he once had for an independent Ukraine to the new soviet republic. He was a socialist and a Ukrainian. I was neither. Little Russia. Ukraine. Ukrainian Socialist Soviet Republic. These were just names to me. My village was as close as I ever came to having a country.

I never told Yuriy that hearing Russian on the streets of Kyiv made me less homesick. Helped me settle in our new life.

I found work as a seamstress in a dress shop. A shop that had fallen on hard times, the clientele it once served now scattered across Europe. Madame Saint-Germain, the owner, claimed she was French but I could tell she was Polish from the way she spoke Russian.

She hired me because I could embroider but kept me busy running up simple frocks on a sewing machine. I preferred sewing by hand but I got used to it.

Sometimes at the end of the day, I would take down a bolt of silk or velvet and unroll it on the long narrow table, my fingers lingering over the material, like a pianist caressing the keys on someone else's piano. I never asked her how she had managed to hold on to so much fabric. Why her shop had no sign of damage anywhere. Why it had never been looted. I didn't want to know.

When the owner couldn't pay me in rubles, she gave me fabric, ribbon, thread, the scissors that had once belonged to her best seamstress. She shared the food she received for the cheaper dresses. That's mostly what we turned out. Simple grey or navy frocks, not unlike the one I wore at the convent in Poltava. Although that was about to change.

Prosperity was seeping back into the city. More goods were appearing in the markets and in the store windows. Shuttered shops were reopening. Restaurants and cafés were adding more tables.

One day a young woman came in with a fashion magazine from Moskva and asked if Madame could make her a dress like the one on the cover. I only make respectable dresses, Madame replied, pushing the magazine back across the counter. Several other women came into the shop with the same request and were turned away.

One evening I stopped at a news kiosk on the way home and asked the man if he had any fashion magazines from Moskva.

"A fashion magazine? Now what would you want with a fashion magazine?" he railed at me, his breath sour, his eyes bleak. "What about the revolution? How can you even think about a new frock when there are people without shelter, without food?"

I hurried away, ashamed that I had asked for something so frivolous.

That night I saw a woman wearing the dress at the tearoom on the ground floor of our apartment building. It was red, calf length, short-sleeved, without a waist or collar. No buttons that I could see. I would have liked to sketch it but the woman wearing it was surrounded by admirers.

I was alone in the shop the next time a customer came in with the magazine. I asked her to leave it with me so I could look over the sewing instructions inside.

The dress on the cover was similar to the one I had seen at the tearoom, except for the sleeves. I went over the sewing instructions. "We could easily make these and for less than other shops," I told Madame when she returned, "with all the fabric you have just sitting here. Fabric that's already paid for."

She ignored the instructions I had laid out on the counter and disappeared into her tiny office with the ledger. When I went home that night, I took the muslin Madame had given me to make a mock-up of the dress, pinning it on the daughter of a neighbour.

The next morning, I went into the shop early. Madame Saint-Germain had given me a key in the winter so I could get the stove going before she arrived and had never asked for it back. I ran up the seams of the muslin on the sewing machine and hemmed it by hand. Draped it over the dummy in the fitting room.

Madame was so angry when she saw it, she swore in Polish and waved her scissors at the mannequin.

"If you destroy it, I'll just make another and I will take it to the shop across the street. We need customers, Madame. We need to move with the times."

But I had already won. I could see it on her face.

Our version of the dress became so popular Madame was able to hire another seamstress and pay us both in rubles, not that they were worth very much. Yuriy didn't approve of the dress or my job in a fancy shop. It was Lenin who had instituted the New Economic Policy to encourage private trade, I reminded him, but he didn't approve of the NEP either.

When the dress shop across the street tried to lure me away, Madame Saint-Germain raised my wages. One of Yuriy's friends, an actor he had met at the Writers' and Artists' Club, found me work sewing costumes for a theatre company and several filmmakers. There was no money in it but I got to see the plays for free. With the filmmakers I learned to ask for the money up front and sometimes I got some.

Here I am in the shop. Wearing a dress of my own creation. With whitework at the hem and at the bottom of the sleeves. Shoes that Madame Saint-Germain wore in her youth.

My hair is short and I've embroidered my lips red for I started to wear lipstick back then, not French lipstick, but some imitation imported from China.

I first saw Mitka in the arms of his sister although I thought at the time she was his mother. They had the same eyes, the colour of dark honey, the same elfin faces. They were dressed in rags, barefoot, and hungry. I saw them every day near the shop. I brought them bread and milk. Sewed a shirt and short pants for the boy, gave the young woman the shoes Madame had given me.

"What's your name?" I asked one day when I realized she would never volunteer it.

"Larissa."

"And your son?"

"My brother. Dmitriy."

"How old is he?"

"Three and a half."

She walked away, annoyed by my questions.

One day the girl entered the shop while I was sewing on the machine in the back room. I heard Madame yelling over the noise the treadle was making and rushed into the store to see what was happening. The girl was already gone.

"Did you give my shoes to that girl?"

"Yes."

"How dare you? After I –"

"I was only being as generous as you were to me, Madame."

She refused to be mollified. "I don't want that girl or her bastard in my shop again!"

The boy is her brother, I wanted to tell her, but I knew she wouldn't believe me.

I didn't see Larissa again for a week. Since she knew where I worked, I started to come to the shop earlier, rattling the iron shutter before I pushed it up, taking my time, giving her plenty of opportunity to approach me.

Another week passed. Then, one morning, the boy was suddenly there, beside me. His dirty thumb in his mouth. I turned to see his sister disappear down a side street. We never saw her again.

This is Mitka standing in the middle of the street, barefoot, wearing the shirt and pants I made for him. He's not smiling or crying.

You can see Madame Saint-Germain's shop behind him and the cake shop next door.

I've embroidered his beautiful eyes, his tangled curls, the crucifix his sister had left in his back pocket. A crucifix that must have belonged to his mother.

Kyiv flourished under the New Economic Policy.

More shops reopened. More merchandise appeared in the market.

Yuriy and his friends objected to the profiteering.

Lenin died.

Yuriy and his friends worried about who would succeed him.

Madame worried about her shop.

I only worried about Mitka.

When Yuriy could finally teach school in Ukrainian, he was ecstatic. His students at the gymnasium less so. They wanted to finish their education in the language they had always learned in. After two frustrating years, Yuriy applied to teach at the primary level.

I went home to take care of my dying father and Vanya's sick wife. Vanya was struggling to keep the farm going. Kostya and Yaroslav were still drinking and gambling, getting into fights in the village. Foma would have driven them out long ago.

I took Mitka home with me, to the cabin by the woods. Mitka went hunting and fishing with Yakiv and Pavlo's boys, swam in the creek, roamed the countryside. No one knew about Mitka's origins. People assumed he'd been born to me and I didn't contradict them.

Mitka fell under the spell of Father Stepan and Ahnesa Andriyivna, as Mitya and I had done. He loved their house, the specimens, the piles of books, the drawings everywhere, the half-finished icons and embroideries.

Tato talked incessantly, he who had always been so silent. He slept in Mama's healing room and I found it hard to sit there without missing her. He died after I had been there a month and we buried him beside his parents and brothers. My sister-in-law died a week later. I didn't tell Vanya she wanted to be buried beside her first husband in the next village.

"Let me stay here another month," Mitka begged when I started to pack.

"Please? Titka said I could stay with them and help her with Uncle Bohdan. He gets so agitated when she leaves the house and I know how to calm him."

Mitka was less scrawny, his skin golden instead of sickly white. It would have been cruel to take him back to our room in someone else's flat, to the heat of the city in August. So I let him stay until school started up again.

Stalin triumphed.

The New Economic Policy was replaced by the First Five Year Plan.

Madame closed down her shop and returned to Krakow.

Yuriy accepted a job in Kharkiv with the People's Commissariat of Education to monitor the progress of Ukrainization in rural schools. Since he would have to absent himself for long periods of time, Mitka and I returned to the village, to the cabin by the woods. I started to teach at the school although I had no training. The teacher wanted to retire and had been waiting for a replacement for two years.

One day when I was sitting outside the cabin, mending Mitka's pants (he had to climb every fence and tree, like Marusiya), a wagon pulled up on the road. I didn't pay attention, I wasn't expecting anyone and I wanted to finish my mending before it got dark.

It was Mama.

News of her arrival spread quickly and before I had set a place for her at the table, a crowd had gathered at our door. I could see how tired Mama was from her journey so I sent them away, knowing they'd be back.

Even more villagers showed up the next day. Ready to build her a treatment room next to my cabin to entice her to stay.

Life was slowly returning to normal.

But it was not meant to be. The revolution wasn't over.

The peasants had yet to be conquered, their farms collectivized.

Yuriy left his job in Kharkiv and came to teach in our village. He wouldn't tell me why he'd left his job at the Commissariat and I didn't press him, grateful to have him back with us. The village children now had a proper teacher and I was free to help Mama with her healing practice.

I started to embroider the pages for this book. It was Ahnesa Andriyivna who first suggested the project. Every day I plied Mama with questions and she answered me in great detail, she who had never told me much about her life or my early years. She was beside me, under the large oak tree, while I pulled the needle through the first cloth page.

Here is Yuriy, teaching at the village school. He has written a poem on the blackboard for the children to memorize. A Ukrainian poem by Shevchenko or Lesya Ukrainka.

Mitka is looking out the window. It's not that he doesn't like poetry, or his father's teaching, but that he would rather be outside. He's like Mitya that way.

I've embroidered large windows, instead of the school's small and dingy ones, so you can see the sky outside and the steppe.

Yuriy attended the meetings about collectivization although we didn't own any fields. He tried to warn the more prosperous farmers that their fields and houses would be confiscated, that they would be deported. He had seen it happen in the many villages he had visited for the Commissariat of Education. No one believed him.

My family's farm, although no longer prosperous, was one of the first to be seized.

My three brothers were deported the same day.

Yuriy was arrested for criticizing collectivization.

Here is Mama lying under the oak tree where she had given birth to me. At the edge of the field that no longer belongs to our family but to the collective. She wanted to die there so Mitka and

I took her every morning in a handcart before we joined the communal harvesting. I've embroidered her with her head on Mitka's lap but she was alone when she died.

Yuriy was sentenced to ten years without right of correspondence.
Father Stepan was arrested.
Our church was ransacked and used to store grain.
A factory worker from Moskva by the name of Zaytsev ran the collective. He divided the village into hundreds, tens and fives, as mandated by Stalin. There were meetings almost every night and we had to participate.

I enlarged the root cellar so I could fill it with more vegetables from my garden and whatever I could buy at the market. I bought extra grain from strangers who passed through our village, without knowing where it had come from. Everyone was nervous about their store of grain under the new system.

Here is Ahnesa Andriyivna embroidering by the window.
There is an icon of the Holy Mother of God on the wall. A pile of books at her feet. A linen frame with several butterflies pinned to it, propped on a shelf.
My face is at the window. My six-year-old face. Lesya is standing behind me but I've embroidered her the age she was when I last saw her instead of the age she was when she first took me to the priest's house.

They don't just want our farms.
They want our grain. All of it.
Won't let us keep enough to feed ourselves.

They find and confiscate my last bit of grain, in spite of my pleadings.

I have nothing to feed my son.

Here is Mitka running across the meadow with the kite his Uncle Bohdan made for him. My brother can't remember the names of his children but can still make a kite, build a chest, carve a toy soldier.

Mitka's hair is as long and curly as a girl's. I've used the last bit of the yellow thread Mama dyed years ago.

The meadow is lush, the sky a crisp blue.

I haven't prayed since I was seventeen.

I offer up my life and Yuriy's.

Mitka dies anyway.

This is the view from the bluff. It's early morning and there is fog on the river. The valley is green, a green so vivid it hurts your eyes.

I wanted the view from the bluff for my title page. It was where I first imagined the world. But I can't embroider the page, my fingers are too swollen, my arms too weak.

I have to imagine it instead. The needle solid between my fingers, the thread tickling my palm, the fabric sighing as I pull the needle through.

I stand at the edge of the bluff.

The fog has burned off.

The river is bright with light.

I am falling.

Falling.

I am not afraid.

ànhel	angel
Baba	grandmother
horilka	liquor distilled from wheat or rye
hustka	shawl
kovbasa	a pork and beef sausage
kvitka	flower
malo solovéy	little nightingale
mandrivnyk	a wanderer
Moskva	Moscow
rushnyk (pl. rushnyky)	ritual towel used for births, weddings, funerals, but also an everyday towel used to wipe one's hands or wrap around a loaf of bread
Tato	father
Titka	aunt
verst	distance, around a kilometre
vesnianka (pl. vesnianky)	spring song
vyshivanka	peasant blouse
whitework	white embroidery on white fabric
znakharka	healer

ONE STEP AT A TIME
IS GOOD WALKING

I sing a sad song, instead of weeping
Stare into the distance, instead of returning
Thinking of my homeland, so many memories
I want to go back, but no one is home
I want to cross the river, but there is no boat
I cannot utter the thoughts in my heart
My belly churns like grinding wheels.

YUE-FU
NINETEEN ANCIENT POEMS
HAN DYNASTY (202 BCE — 220 CE)

THE DUST FROM THE DEMOLITION hangs in the air like smoke, the noise of the wrecking ball as steady as the artillery that once pounded the city walls. Half-destroyed buildings, piles of rubble, and the remnants of a foundation crowd into my viewfinder, masquerading as the ruins of sixty years ago. It's as if the past were trying to rematerialize in front of me, to fill my eyes and ears with what I have failed to imagine.

Not so much a déja vu as a jamais vu since I was already in a refugee camp in Hong Kong when the Japanese invaded Nanjing. Since I was no longer living on Taiping Lu when soldiers destroyed every shop on the street, including my father's ink store and the two rooms at the back that were our home.

I scan the construction site, avoiding the crane and the excavator, and focus on the three buildings that are still intact, the sunlight trapped in their dirty windows. I press the shutter release, wind the film forward and take another shot, the last one on the roll. The film is black and white, as if I can't trust the old Leica to handle colour.

Taiping Lu.

Nothing is left of the street but the name.

Even the dimensions of it have changed: the street is wider, the blocks are longer and the maze of back alleys has disappeared. I can't pinpoint where *The Four Treasures* once stood but I have narrowed it down to this block which is being demolished to make way for a hotel and shopping complex.

There is a sudden lull in the construction noise as the workers stop for lunch. Other sounds rush in, car horns, bicycle bells, the clang of bamboo scaffolding being dismantled. Sounds that seem soft, almost musical, after all that pounding.

I lean against a concrete drain pipe at the edge of the site and wipe the sweat off my face and neck with a handkerchief. There is dust on my hair and skin and clothes.

The past has retreated. The chunks of concrete, the bricks, the splintered wood have morphed back into demolition debris.

I feel nothing.

All the emotion I expected to feel, I dreaded to feel, once I arrived in China, has still not manifested itself.

When I return to the hotel, I stop by the fitness centre where Helen is swimming laps to relieve her jet lag. I watch her for a while, the blue of her bathing suit indistinguishable from the water, her limbs small and white. I love her energy, her stamina, the way she moves through the water. Through Life.

Back in our room, I sit on the unmade bed, too tired to change out of my dusty clothes. Next to me, on the night table, is the red notebook Jing Mei thrust into my hands at the airport. Write down your story, Yeye, she said. Write down your story.

Yeye. Jing Mei is the only one of my grandchildren who calls me that. The only one who answers to a Chinese name, a name she crafted for herself, to replace the Jennifer Marie her parents had given her.

The notebook she gave me is garish, the faux-silk cover strewn with thick Chinese characters. The calligraphy, if you can call it that, would have upset Wu Jiao; the cheap paper would have made my father shudder. Is it garish on purpose, another rebuke from Jing Mei, for not being Chinese enough?

I stretch out on the bed although Helen has warned me not to take a nap, that it will only make the jet lag worse.

Write down your story. A simple enough request, like send me a postcard or take lots of pictures. I was returning to the country of my birth after all. What could be more natural?

I drift off before Helen slips her keycard into the lock.

It is the middle of the night and I can't sleep. I am paying dearly for my nap now, just as Helen predicted. She should know, always off on some trip with the Teachers' Federation, touring with strangers because her friends have husbands who love to travel and she doesn't.

"Where are you going?" Helen asks. I can smell the chlorine in her hair as she lifts her head off the pillow.

"Down to the lobby. I can't sleep."

She rubs my back. Doesn't say I told you so.

I take the stairs instead of the elevator. The lobby is deserted except for an American gentleman ensconced in a leather chair, his booted feet on the coffee table, reading the Wall Street Journal. Our eyes meet.

Why didn't I grab Jing Mei's notebook as I was leaving or one of Helen's many guidebooks? Anything to pass the time. Maybe I can strike up a conversation with the American, find out where he's from, what kind of business he's in. I used to love talking to strangers. But the newspaper is slack now, the American is asleep, snoring with his mouth open.

I walk over to the front desk and ask the young man on duty for some stationery. He doesn't smile or make eye contact, just hands me a few sheets of paper and an ugly postcard of the hotel. As I settle in the chair across from the American, who is snoring more loudly now, I grab a magazine with a pink peony on the cover to use as a writing surface. I uncap my fountain pen, a gift from my children when I retired from teaching.

They say you never forget your mother tongue but I'm not so sure.
Tongues can be cut out.
Words can die in your throat and lodge there, useless.
Like fossils.

The words surprise me, their sharp edges slicing through more than the cheap paper.

We are travelling to Suzhou to see the gardens. A two and a half hour train ride, long enough to get a narrative going, although all I've produced so far is a lapful of crumpled paper. I'm glad I bought a legal pad at the hotel's business centre, that I left the garish notebook in our hotel room.

"Just write, Michael. Let it flow. You can always edit later," Helen suggests, without lifting her eyes from her guidebook. This is the first time she has alluded to Jing Mei's request although the notebook has been lying around the room for three days. I even thought Helen was behind the idea since she used to ask her students to interview their grandparents as part of her history syllabus. But she and Jing Mei are no longer close. Not since the girl changed her name and became more Chinese than the Chinese.

I learned my first English words on a train, deep in the mountains of Jiangxi Province. We had coasted to a stop on a desolate stretch of track. A rockslide, the old man wheezed. A washed out bridge, argued another. We've run out of coal again, grumbled someone else. There was no end to the speculation. I held my breath but no one wailed, no one tried to jump off the train. I scanned the rock face for Japanese soldiers anyway, the sky (the little I could see of it) for a bomber squadron. Just because no one was panicking didn't mean we were safe.

Let me teach you some English, Miss Rutherford suggested in her clumsy Mandarin. We were headed for Hong Kong, where people spoke Cantonese or English and wouldn't be able to understand me. How do you say Japanese soldier, I asked, as I turned my back on what was lurking outside. Forget about the Japanese, she said, I want to teach you something useful.

So what could be more useful than knowing the name of your enemy?

The first word Miss Rutherford tried to teach me was rice. She isolated the sound of each letter, revving the r-r-r at the back of her throat.

(Don't forget I didn't know what a letter was, let alone the letter r). Rice, rice, rice, she repeated as she pretended to eat from a bowl, holding her imaginary chopsticks like only a foreigner would. The word that rolled off my tongue didn't sound like hers, no matter how many times I tried.

I should have started with something easier, she said, as she sipped from an invisible cup, blowing into it to cool the contents. Teee, she chanted, holding the cup aloft. Teee, teee, teee!

The men across from us were watching and listening intently.

Teee, they repeated, when I failed to take my cue. Teee, they squealed, lifting imaginary cups to their lips and slurping. Others crowded around us and laughed, tossing the strange word in the air like a juggling stick. Teee! Teee!

Miss Rutherford ignored them and continued her lesson with the word fish. Opening and closing her mouth, making swimming motions with her hands. Fishhh, she hissed, her lips pushing together in an exaggerated pucker. Fishhh. The men laughed louder. I didn't repeat the word or look at her, embarrassed by all the attention we were getting. She sighed in exasperation and returned to her book. It would soon be too dark to read.

What is my name in English, I asked her later, when the train shuddered back to life. Shan means mountain, she replied, but people would still call you Shan.

I peered out the grimy window. I could no longer see the mountains but I could feel them shifting in the darkness, like dragons settling down for the night. Would my father have called me Shan if he had known how many mountains would one day come between us?

By the time our train reached Hong Kong, days late, Miss Rutherford had taught me many English words. Words that tasted bland and doughy in my mouth, like steamed buns without the filling, except for the word sing, which had a whiff of red bean paste to it.

She tried to find a family I could live with – her ship was sailing for England in less than a week – but Hong Kong was overrun with refugees and she had to place me in a camp. She came to visit me twice before she left, bringing me food and warmer clothes (which were quickly grabbed by the bullies in my tent), and a shabby English dictionary at the front of which she had sketched her dispensary and Wu Jiao's table, and on the back cover, my father's shop. I didn't notice the drawings until after she had gone so I was never able to thank her properly or tell her how much they meant to me.

On the second visit, Miss Rutherford introduced me to Mrs. Milner, a Chinese woman in spite of her name, who ran the clinic at the camp and taught English to the refugees. The nurse greeted me warmly and encouraged me to join her class. I just wanted the two women to leave before the bullies came back.

When I didn't show up in the days that followed, Mrs. Milner came looking for me. Eileen asked me to take care of you, she explained in Mandarin. Come, the class starts in a few minutes. As I followed her that dreary morning, the mud grabbing at my feet (the bullies having taken my shoes), I had no idea how long a journey it would turn out to be.

Helen has fallen asleep beside me, the guidebook open on her lap, her thin highlighter like a cigarette between her fingers. I don't know if she wants me to wake her, if jet lag is still a concern. I cover her with my sweater instead.

Life in the camp was grim, except for Mrs. Milner's class. English was my future, I realized, even as I picked up enough Cantonese to get by. I had nothing to lose. The brutes had already taken everything, including Miss Rutherford's dictionary and the scroll my father had slipped into my bag at the last minute.

One day Mrs. Milner returned the dictionary to me, its front cover almost falling off. I believe this is yours, she said. I picked it up at one of the stalls outside the camp. She pointed to Miss Rutherford's sketch inside the front cover. I worked at that dispensary with Eileen many years ago, she continued, when my husband was with the British Embassy in Nanjing.

I asked her to keep the dictionary for me. I didn't know enough English to use it and I didn't want it to fall in the hands of my tormentors.

The drawings were safe. I found comfort in that and in knowing that Mrs. Milner had once worked close to my home on Taiping Lu. That she had known Wu Jiao. That we might have walked by each other in the market or on the street.

Mrs. Milner taught us simple words, everyday words, and often brought something tangible to help us remember them. We learned the words for orange, mango, and lychee with a piece of fruit in our mouth. The word for hat while passing her husband's old cap around. We brought her water, mud, leaves, seeds, whatever we could find, so we could learn their English equivalents.

Orange was my favourite English word. I liked the weight and feel of it on my tongue. Every time I scratched it in the dirt, my mouth watered for the oranges Mama used to peel for Baba and me.

Mrs. Milner eventually taught us the alphabet, printing the letters, one at a time, on a slate we passed around. Most of her students didn't know how to read or write. I was one of the few who did. The number of letters in one word surprised me as I was used to characters and strokes and radicals.

Years later, when I was sitting in your father's first grade class, waiting to talk to his teacher, I noticed the letters of the alphabet she had printed at the top of the blackboard and I was so overwhelmed I rushed out of the room and stumbled down a hallway decorated with cut-outs for Hallowe'en.

Mrs. Milner taught us how to write our names, to invert their order. I liked the first letter of my name, the S like a snake, a dragon, a curving river.

I asked Mrs. Milner to write down the words for my favourite dishes on a piece of paper so I could practise writing them with a stick in the dirt. Salt fish and pickled mustard greens. Cabbage and fresh bean curd. Spicy pork. Rice. I imagined each dish, the way it looked and smelled and tasted. And every time I wrote rice or fish, I thought of Miss Rutherford and the words she taught me on the train.

Mrs. Milner cut our hair, got rid of our lice, gave us the clothes and shoes she had collected from other British families. Brought us soap, candles, and matches.

My English improved once I started helping Mrs. Milner at the clinic. The line-ups were long and the medical supplies few but I was eager for something to do. I fetched water, scrounged for firewood, ripped cloth to make bandages. Mrs. Milner taught me how to clean and dress a wound, prepare a poultice, calm a sick baby.

A man comes by pushing a trolley, selling tea, snacks, fruits, and newspapers. Helen is still sleeping. I buy two oranges and two styrofoam cups of tea but when I tell him to keep the change, I look down instead of up. I'm ashamed of my clothes here, my good shoes, the money in my wallet.

In November 1939, after I had been in the camp for two years, Mrs. Milner told me that her husband was retiring from the Army and they were emigrating to Canada.

I looked down at my feet as she spoke, at the shoes she had just given me. Shoes one of the bullies would be wearing before the day was out. Even if I smeared them with mud.

Would you like to come with us, Shan?

I went over the words I had learned about shoes in my head. Leather, sole, heel, laces. Shoeshine.

Those are my son's shoes, she said. And the shirt you are wearing used to be his also. Michael is younger than you are but tall for his age. He takes after his father.

I could feel the weight of each word in my ear.

There is war in Europe, she continued, and we don't know how long it will last. With England distracted, the Japanese will attack Hong Kong and when they do, you won't be safe.

Her son was at school in England. He was the one she should be worrying about.

Think about it, Shan.

I thought about nothing else for days. I was sick of the camp, the terrible food, the beatings, the crushing loneliness. But how could I leave when I didn't know what had happened to my parents, when I had only received one letter from my father, dated before the Japanese entered Nanjing? When I didn't know if the rumours of a massacre were true?

Mrs. Milner waited a week before asking me again, in English this time. I told her I would go with them. I knew my parents would have wanted me to leave – they had been so adamant about getting me out of Nanjing – but the decision weighed heavily on me just the same. A good son would never abandon his parents.

I moved in with the Milners. I slept in their son's bed. Wore his clothes, read his books, ate at his place at the table. Because his son was still listed on his passport, the Major was able to arrange my passage to Canada under Michael's name. Luckily, I was small enough and pale enough to pass as a fourteen-year-old Eurasian.

I never answered to Wang Shan again.

Fate changed my name but my father changed both his name and his fate. He started calling himself Ah Fu, which means lucky, when

he was sixteen. Some of that luck had rubbed off on me. Spiriting
me out of Nanjing before the Japanese entered the city in 1937, out of
Hong Kong before it fell, and into Canada which still had a ban on
Chinese immigration.

Baba's luck and the kindness of strangers.

I thread the cap back on the pen, leave the pages on my seat
for Helen to read. She is awake now and eating her orange, her
face to the window. When I return from stretching my legs,
the pages are still there, undisturbed. She will not read my
account unless I ask her and even then, she might refuse. It's as
if the parcel that arrived from Hong Kong four months ago were
crammed between our seats, as if we had lugged it back across the
Pacific Ocean.

Outside the train station in Suzhou, I choose the scrawniest pedicab driver, a habit that annoys my wife. When I explain that we
need him for the whole day, that we want him to take us from one
garden to the other, the man smiles so broadly and bobs his head
so vigorously, it sharpens the pain in my gut. I think pedicabs are
barbaric but this man needs money, not pity.

Helen climbs into the shabby cab without complaining. She
is economical that way. Never voices an objection more than once.
The opposite of a nag. She hands me the list of the gardens she
wants to see and the order in which she wants to see them. I climb
in beside her and ask the driver to take us to the Garden of the
Master of the Nets.

We travel down the main thoroughfare for a long time before
we turn onto a narrow street. The farther down that street we go,
the narrower it gets and the more apprehensive Helen becomes. I
can tell by the way she grips her guidebook. She thinks the man is

lost or worse, out to rob us. When he finally comes to a stop and wipes the sweat off his face, he points proudly to a gate and a small sign. *Wangshiyuan*.

As soon as we have bought our tickets, Helen walks away from me, her nose in her guidebook. She will read about each pavilion, each element of the garden – it's the history teacher in her, she can't help it. I wander around without reading anything, trusting that the garden will reveal itself to me as it was designed to do.

I settle on a pavilion that projects over the pond and sit there, my eyes roaming over the water, the lily pads, the cypresses and junipers. The stones pretending to be mountains.

I am sitting in Wangshiyuan, the Garden of the Master of the Nets, the smallest and most exquisite of the many gardens in Suzhou (according to Major Milner and the guidebook your grandmother is reading). I will take a picture from where I sit so you can appreciate the beauty that surrounds me as I write this. I'm using Major Milner's old Leica rangefinder (thanks to your brother who rerolled film onto spools that fit the camera).

Major Milner. He was as blustery as his wife was shy. A big man with a red face, big hands and feet. He took charge of my education from the moment we set sail for Canada, drilling me like an army recruit. Once we reached Vancouver, he set off to explore his new city, traipsing for hours every day, dragging me along every weekend. He ignored the people who stared at us.

They think you're inferior, he told me once, but you're not. That's all you need to know.

He enrolled me in the high school down the street from the bungalow he had bought, which seemed palatial to me at the time. Placed me in a grade nine class with fourteen year olds and continued to tutor me in all subjects. No one at the school realized how old I was or that the Milners were not my parents (the Major had used his son's birth certificate to register me). When my classmates asked me where I was from, I stuck to the lie that had allowed me into the country: that my father, an officer in the British Army, had retired to Canada after many years in Hong Kong.

I spoke English even when Mrs. Milner sent me to Chinatown on an errand. I ignored the Chinese kids I encountered at school, including a girl I fancied, and preferred Christmas and Easter over the Chinese New Year, although I never told Mrs. Milner this.

Improving my English was my only obsession, while yours, Jing Mei, is to improve your Mandarin, a language your parents refused to learn. How strange is that?

The Major encouraged me to read the newspaper, to borrow books from the library, to look up every word I didn't know in his big, leather-bound dictionary, a retirement gift from his regiment. (I preferred Miss Rutherford's dictionary but kept it in my room to spare his feelings.) I relied on the radio for slang and practised in front of the mirror. Okay. Sure. Yeah. Gee Whiz. See you later.

I studied harder than my friends and earned money making deliveries for a pharmacy and a small grocery with my bike. At school, I was never allowed to forget I was Chinese but after the bombing of Pearl Harbour and the fall of Hong Kong, it was much worse. How do we know you're not a Jap, the kids kept asking me. Chinks, Japs – you all look the same with those ugly slits you call eyes.

I ignored them when they called me a Chink or half-a-Chink, Yellow Face, Pigtail, but I would not let them call me a Jap. I often came home with a bloody nose. Major Milner visited my class, in his Army uniform, with his medals from the First War pinned to his chest, but the kids were not impressed.

The Major enrolled me in a new school, where the majority of the students were Chinese, but it was only marginally better. Now my English name and my being half-Chinese were an issue (which was ironic, given that I wasn't). The school was much farther away so the long bus ride there and back prevented me from making new friends or maintaining the ones I already had.

After high school, it took me several tries to get accepted at the Normal School (I was ready to give up but the Major always persuaded me to try again). It was the interview that gave me the most trouble, the discrepancy between the name on the application and my Chinese face. When I was finally accepted and after I obtained my teaching certificate, the only job I could find was in a small mill town near Abbotsford.

As I take pictures of the Humble Administrator's Garden with Major Milner's camera, I am not thinking of him but of his son, my namesake, although namesake no longer seems honest. Did the-real-Michael ever bring his two daughters to Suzhou? Did he stand here, in this garden, and take their picture with the Leica I now hold in my hands?

I'm ashamed that I never contacted him after Mrs. Milner died. That I never offered my condolences or expressed my gratitude for the small legacy she had left me. That I never told him that his parents' kindness is engraved in my bones.

I don't understand why he remembered me when he was putting his own affairs in order. Why he asked his daughters to send me the Leica, the jade pendant Mrs. Milner always wore, and the photo albums that chronicled the Milners' years in Vancouver. I didn't deserve any consideration.

When the box first arrived from Hong Kong, I hid it in the basement. I had no idea what it contained nor did I recognize the name of the person who had sent it to me. It had to be about Michael. Who else did I know in Hong Kong?

I waited until Helen went away on a quilting weekend before I brought the box up again and opened it. There was a note and an obituary from the Times tucked into one of the albums. *Our father thought you might like to have these mementoes of his parents. He died in his sleep on January 1, 1997, six months to the day before Hong Kong is to be handed back to China. He was a proud British Hong Konger to the end. Yours sincerely, Sarah Milner Hobbes and Elizabeth Milner Yee.*

I was disappointed that the note was so brief but what more could they have written? To a man they had never met, who lived on the other side of the world, a man who bore their father's name?

When Helen returned from her quilting weekend, I showed her the camera and the photo albums and told her that a cousin had sent them. Then I gave her the jade pendant.

"Oh Michael, it's lovely. I can't believe I finally have something of your mother's. Can you help me with the clasp?"

My mother who had never owned a piece of jewelry in her life.

Helen perused the albums, exclaiming every time she found a picture of Mrs. Milner wearing the pendant or recognized a Vancouver landmark.

"Is Shan your Chinese name?"

"Yes, it means mountain."

Helen loved cameras so she also took an interest in the Leica. Which is how she came to find an old business card of Michael's tucked into the case.

Michael Edward Milner
Directorate of Commercial Relations,
Hong Kong Territory

"Your cousin has the same name as you. Were you named after a common grandfather?"

I couldn't focus on the question. The news of Michael's death had shaken me. As had the pendant, the Leica, and the photo albums.

"Michael? It's not that difficult a question."

Everything Helen knew about me was a lie. My name, my age, who my parents were, where I was born, where I grew up.

"My name is Wang Shan," I said.

The Milners returned to Hong Kong in 1947. The Major would have preferred to stay in Vancouver – he loved the city, his garden, their friends – but Mrs. Milner was sick of her life as a Chinese alien. She wanted me to return with them but the Major encouraged me to stay. This is the place to be, he told me one Sunday afternoon, as we strolled through Stanley Park. It won't be easy but Canada is a young country. It will change. It's what your parents would want for you. What I want for you.

I had already decided to stay. After another five years near Abbotsford, I finally secured a teaching job in Vancouver, at the high school where your grandmother had just been hired. I thought I would finally belong, finally blend in, but people still asked me where I was from. Neighbours, the parents of my students, the guy behind the meat counter at Safeway. Even after I got married, even after the birth of my four children. I continued to tell people my father was in the British Army, that he'd married my mother in Hong Kong.

Every time I referred to the Milners, I felt I was betraying my parents. I didn't know what had happened to Baba and Mama and I felt guilty about that too. The Major had written to the Red Cross and Mrs. Milner to officials in Nanjing but we never received any information. I made enquiries after the Japanese withdrew but civil war followed by a repressive regime prevented me from pursuing it any further. I resigned myself to never knowing my parents' fate.

What about your name, people would ask. I would shrug, like Milner was as common in China as Wang, but a shrug was never much use in that kind of conversation. You eventually had to answer or walk away. I learned to walk away. What right do you have to a white name like Michael Milner? they'd yell at my retreating back.

The colour of people, the colour of names, the first lesson I learned in Canada. Mrs. Milner was yellow but her name was white. Major Milner was white although his face was red. Red was for Indians and not the ones from India, who were brown. The prejudice might have been straightforward but the colours were confusing.

Zijin Shan. Purple Mountain. There is this to say about a mountain, it doesn't change. It stands where it has always stood, looks like it has always looked. Well, not quite. Zijin Shan looks more like a hill to me now after years of living in the shadow of the Coast Mountains.

My father used to bring me here when I was a boy, to visit the Ming tombs or the Sun Yat-sen mausoleum. If we were visiting the mausoleum, he would invite Wu Jiao to accompany us, even though he was too old and frail to climb the steps to the burial chamber. Wu Jiao was a public scribe who had befriended my father in his youth. As close to a yeye as I ever had. Wu Jiao was so devoted to Sun Yat-sen, he was content to sit on the bench near the marble archway, his eyes closed, his bony hands on his walking stick, and wait for us to come down again.

Helen and I start up the steps together but she soon tires of my plodding and pulls ahead. It's cool in the shade of the pines and cypresses that have grown so tall since I was last here. I used to run up these steps, getting ahead of my father, and run back down to find him again. Baba would laugh as I reported how many steps I had climbed, how many people I had passed, how many trees I had counted.

My father would often stop and fill his lungs with air and let it out slowly, his eyes closed. I would imitate him, knowing Baba was breathing deeply in memory of his own father who had struggled for breath all his life, who could never have climbed the hundreds of steps to the burial chamber.

So I stop now to inhale deeply, as Baba would have done. My eyes closed.

"What are you doing, Michael? Waiting for someone to knock you down?"

Helen has come back to check on me. She suppresses a sigh but I hear it anyway. I should tell her about my grandfather. His bad lungs. But I don't know how to talk to her about my past in spite of everything I have set down on paper for Jing Mei. We resume our slow ascent. Helen tries to stay with me, to talk to me, but my silence drives her away again.

When I reach the burial chamber, she is already taking pictures of the sarcophagus. It bothers me that she has brought her Nikon to China. We even had words about it. I understand why you won't buy a Japanese camera, she told me, but yours is German. From the thirties. Probably made by slave labour. Does that not bother you? I didn't respond as the Leica was too closely connected to the unmasking of my past.

I lean on the railing to look down at the reclining figure of Sun Yat-sen, the white marble a little dingy in the artificial light. I remember my father leaning against this railing and wonder if my mother ever came here, if her eyes ever rested on the great man carved in stone.

When we leave the burial chamber, we find pictures of Sun Yat-sen's funeral on display on an outside wall. Helen photographs the pictures, one after another. For Jing Mei, who is a great admirer of this man. Even though she and Jing Mei are no longer close.

"I watched the funeral procession," I force myself to tell her. Might as well start with something interesting, something that will appeal to the historian in her.

She lowers the camera and stares at me, astonished. "You watched the funeral procession of Sun Yat-sen?"

I nod.

"And you were how old?"

"Eight."

We walk down together, Helen holding on to my arm. She doesn't mention the funeral again but I know she will grill me later.

Your grandmother and I are staying at a hotel on Zhongshan Lu, a road that reaches back into my childhood. The building of this road was such a huge project, hundreds of houses and shops had to be torn down to make way for it. The work crews started at the river's edge in the north, cut diagonally through the city, and turned east to the base of Purple Mountain where Sun Yat-sen's tomb was being built.

I had two friends my age, Yuying and Zhao. Yuying's family ran the hot-water shop in an alley off Taiping Lu and Zhao's parents, the tailor shop next to The Four Treasures. The three of us were obsessed with the building of Zhongshan Lu. We watched as the houses and shops were being demolished, feeling none of the dismay our parents felt for those who were being displaced. Awed instead by the vistas that were opening up. It was like standing on the Zhonghua Gate and looking down on the city spread out below.

When the paving crews reached the edge of our neighbourhood, we ran down every day to watch them work. We had never seen asphalt before. Or a road so wide. Or a road lined on both sides with trees. I can see those trees from our hotel room, plane trees, I think they are called. Two green ribbons unrolling through the city for kilometres. I hope the trees will survive all the tearing down and construction that is going on in Nanjing now.

Zhongshan Lu had to be ready for Sun Yat-sen's funeral procession. He'd been dead close to four years and they were only burying him now. Zhao said there were only bones left to bury but Yuying claimed the body had been preserved like Lenin's (I didn't know where Yuying got this information or who Lenin was). I would've asked Wu Jiao if Sun Yat-sen's body was intact but he was so devoted to him that I didn't dare pose such a delicate question.

On the day of the funeral procession, all the shops were forced to close and people thronged both sides of the new road. There were flags everywhere, blue with a white sunburst, the symbol of the Nationalist party. Wu Jiao got me one of the badges they were handing out, also blue with the sunburst, and pinned it to my jacket. It was a new jacket Mama had made for me from a remnant of dark-blue sateen Zhao's father had given her. A jacket that made the hot day seem even hotter.

We waited a long time for the procession to reach our part of town. The crowd was getting restless, spilling out onto the new road before being pushed back. Finally the first soldiers appeared, on horseback. Followed by policemen. More soldiers, rows and rows of them, on foot this time. A torrent of people and banners flowed by, splashing us with colour and noise. Peasants, university students, dignitaries, schoolchildren in uniform, men and women representing every part of the country.

There were many marching bands and they all played the Burial Song, which had been composed for the occasion, and which we were to hum for months afterwards.

We stared at our first foreigners, men in funny suits and top hats, others in turbans. When the casket finally came into view, I was on Baba's shoulders and I could see it very well but the glass top was covered in flags and silks so I couldn't see the body.

You are a witness to history, Wu Jiao told me when the procession had passed and the crowd was thinning. It is your duty to remember this day, to tell your sons and grandsons that you watched the funeral procession of the great Sun Yat-sen.

I never mentioned it to anyone, not even my wife. Wu Jiao would have been ashamed of me. He could not know that there would be a massacre on the road they had built to honour his hero. That my children and grandchildren would be born far from Nanjing, far from China.

Jing Mei will scold me for not telling her about Sun Yat-sen's funeral. Just as she scolds me for not being Chinese enough. Wu Jiao would have loved her. The fiercest of my grandchildren.

My Baba was the last child of a struggling family. His father was a ricksha puller with bad lungs; his mother sold eggs on the street. After his father died, his mother went to live with his older brother and Baba had to fend for himself. He slept wherever he could, in the train station, under a market stall, in the fields, because there were still fields within the city walls back then.

He was always on the look out. If a fruit rolled off a wagon or a few sticks dropped off a cart, he'd be the first to scoop them up. If someone had an errand, he was ready to run it and usually not for money. He delivered letters for the public scribes in the market in exchange for reading lessons. Lugged coal for people so he could borrow their tools. He fixed broken wheels, plugged holes in buckets, mended baskets. Salvaged bricks, roof tiles, pieces of lumber from abandoned buildings.

One day he found a rusty bicycle under a pile of rubble. One of the wheels was bent and although he straightened it, the bicycle remained unsteady. He rode around, offering his services, selling his salvage. He never begged. Remembered everyone by name. Had an uncanny memory for faces and the way people walked.

Wu Jiao, one of the public scribes who taught Baba how to read (and whom I have already mentioned), found him work as a servant for a retired teacher. Old Chen had tutored the sons of a wealthy merchant and received a pension and the use of a small house for the rest of his life. Not the usual fate of tutors, he told Baba proudly. He couldn't afford to pay my father but shared his humble home and meals with him. They would sit on the stoop together and the teacher would recite classic tales – often the same one as his mind was failing – and Baba wouldn't let on, listening in wonder as if he'd never heard it before. Old Chen also taught my father how to do sums and keep accounts.

Baba looked after Old Chen while he continued to scavenge and run errands for other people. He now called himself Ah Fu because he had been lucky enough to find shelter, regular meals, and companionship. When Old Chen died, he inherited his possessions. He sold the chest full of books and gave his mother the money. He offered the ink stone and brushes to Wu Jiao and added the teacher's padded jacket and pants to his own small bundle of belongings.

He left word of Old Chen's passing with the merchant's family and went back to sleeping at the train station. About a week later, when Wu Jiao told him the merchant was looking for him, he went to his office, worried that the books had not been his to sell. He appeared before the merchant in the clothes he'd inherited from Old Chen. The sleeves of the dark blue jacket pushed back, the pants tied with a piece of rope.

The merchant looked him over and asked a few questions. Baba was mumbling and twisting his cap in his hands. When the man offered him work instead of a reprimand, he backed out of the office, unable to believe his good fortune. Unloading coal bricks from river barges was dirty, backbreaking work but my father did it proudly. After two years, the merchant rewarded him with a job in the accounting department.

Old Hong, the head accountant, resented the scrawny young man the merchant had sent him and thought his employer's trust in Ah Fu was misplaced. Baba understood this and patiently recopied all the figures whenever Old Hong found an error, even when he knew the error wasn't his. He went out of his way to treat the accountant with respect. Asked him to clarify entries he understood perfectly well. Pointed out tiny discrepancies in the invoices of their suppliers, a few fen here, a few fen there, amounts that could become significant given the volume of goods that flowed through the merchant's many warehouses. Old Hong stopped trying to discredit him.

After three years, the merchant called my father into his office and asked him what he knew about ink. Baba answered that it was one of the four treasures of the study and the merchant smiled. He'd bought a small ink shop on Taiping Lu called The Four Treasures and wanted Baba to run it for him. He'd have to live in the rooms at the back, the merchant stipulated, as the stock was too valuable to leave unguarded.

Baba had never dreamed of running a store on Taiping Lu, let alone have two rooms to himself. All that time he had spent with public scribes like Wu Jiao and now he was going to sell the tools of their trade.

The merchant also arranged for Baba to marry Jing Wei, the daughter of one of his tenant farmers. She was tiny (Jing Wei means small bird) and past marriageable age, the only daughter of a farmer with many sons.

Her mother had died giving birth to her so she was considered unlucky and mistreated by the family. She was so unhappy she was planning to take rat poison when the merchant arrived to arrange the marriage.

These are the stories Baba told me as I sat on my little stool in the shop, on the crossbar of his bicycle, or as we walked together on the ancient Ming wall.

The sharp, acrid smell of ink grabs the back of my throat, burns the edges of my eyes. I force myself to walk around the store, to examine the ink sticks which are of the finest quality, without any of the garish designs I've seen in the stalls on the street. Too beautiful to break up and use, to choose one over another.

The man behind the counter is not wearing a black apron but a navy suit, a white shirt and a red tie. The cuffs of the shirt are immaculate, his hands clean. He must wear gloves when he handles the ink sticks although I don't see any. He does not smile but affects the indifference I have noticed in store clerks here, although this man is obviously the owner. The man's indifference inhibits me. I should not have come in here alone, I should have waited for Helen. She is so decisive. She would've selected several ink sticks by now, although she knows nothing about them, an ink stone and some brushes. She would have the man rushing around for her. She has that effect on people, even here.

I examine the ink stones on the next counter but there are too many to choose from. Jing Mei was born in the year of the goat but I want something that has a dragon on it, for her fierceness. I keep moving, past the rolls of xuan paper that smell like wet dust, the porcelain pots stuffed with brushes of all kinds.

Brush, ink, paper, ink stone: *the four treasures of the study,* my father's stock-in-trade.

I leave without buying a gift for Jing Mei.

Let me tell you about The Four Treasures on Taiping Lu. By the time I was born, my parents had been selling brushes, ink sticks, parchment and ink stones for nine years and were still living in the two rooms at the back of the shop. My earliest memories are of the shop: the smell of ink in my nose, the black sheen on Baba's hands, the feel of his leather apron against my cheek. My mother's fingers on the abacus, the worry on her wrinkled face.

There were samples of calligraphy hanging everywhere. Poems, proverbs, the wisdom of Confucius, passages from the Tao. I'm afraid I only remember a few of the proverbs. The palest ink is better than the best memory. A closed mind is like a closed book, just a block of wood. A bridge never crossed is a life never lived.

All the calligraphy was brushed by Wu Jiao, my father's old friend, who'd been a civil servant and a scholar before he fell out of favour. He was reduced to writing banners for special celebrations, couplets to hang for the New Year, and letters for people who couldn't write. Wu Jiao had a table in the market and as soon as I was old enough to venture on my own, I spent time with him each day. He is the one who taught me to read and write.

Sometimes I would pretend to be a scribe like Wu Jiao. I would place the four treasures on the table Papa kept outside the store, in the order that Wu Jiao preferred. Unroll the parchment, keeping it flat with two paperweights. Standing still as if I were waiting for the spirit to move me, I would pull the brush from my sleeve, dip it in the inkless inkstone and draw the characters with a flourish. Then I would rest the brush on the inkstone, draw my hands into my sleeves and thank the gods for their inspiration. Wu Jiao caught my little act once and laughed. Never mentioned it to Baba who would've slapped me for being disrespectful.

To this day I can remember the calligraphy that adorned The Four Treasures, the stretch and sweep of Wu Jiao's strokes, the way the parchment curled at the edges. But if I dream of the shop, of my parents standing behind the counter in their worn leather aprons, the four treasures of the study on display, the scrolls that hang all around them are blank.

Helen finishes the last page of what I have written so far and places it, face down, on the pile. She taps the edges of the pages against the desk, to square them off. I knew she would do that. She is always tidying, inserting a little order in the chaos that is the world.

She removes her glasses and looks at me with those blue eyes I love so much, faded now but still round and limpid. The eyes Jing Mei has inherited, much to her chagrin, as they are not Chinese. When I told her once, how I had fallen for her grandmother's eyes, she was not impressed. You are Chinese, she said. How can you love round eyes? They are so unnatural. Like those Anime faces.

I'm afraid that Jing Mei will not like what I have written, that I have not conjured up the past she wants.

"So that dictionary I threw out, was the one Miss Rutherford gave you at the camp? The one with the drawings of her dispensary, of Wu Jiao's table, your father's shop?"

"You couldn't have known –"

"Of course I couldn't have!"

I flinch. Her eyes are hard but filling with tears. She turns her head so I won't see them.

"And you pick scrawny pedicab drivers because your grandfather was a ricksha puller,"

I nod although her face is turned away. Although it wasn't a question. "You have to forgive me, Helen."

She shakes her head, her thick grey hair still damp from her morning swim. "There is nothing to forgive."

"I lied to you. Told you the same story I told everyone who asked me where I was from. Although you were my wife and the mother of my children. Although you deserved the truth and the others didn't."

"The truth is the truth, Michael. It's not something one deserves or doesn't deserve. I was hurt and angry when I found out that everything I knew about you, the little I knew about you, was a lie. When Jing Mei gave you that notebook at the airport, I wanted to rip the shoddy little diary right out of your hands. What right did she have to your story when I had to wait fifty years to hear it? Jing Mei, who is ashamed of me because I'm not Chinese."

I place one hand over hers, smooth her hair back with the other.

"I was wrong, Michael, to make such a fuss. You are the one who was betrayed, the one who lost everyone and everything. Your parents, your friends, your home, your country. I should have focussed on that instead of my hurt feelings. Can you ever forgive me?"

In 1937, Nanjing went through a construction boom that eclipsed the building of Zhongshan Lu eight years earlier. There were so many major construction projects, there was a shortage of labour and better wages than usual. I had no trouble finding work. Wu Jiao had taught me to read and write, my mother to do sums but hard physical labour was what was required. I was sixteen and eager to be a man.

Baba was worried about the Japanese. He'd always had an ear for news and he didn't like what he was hearing. He was convinced the Japanese wanted more than the northern provinces they'd already seized. There was a retired general who came into the shop to buy his ink and who would sometimes engage Baba in conversation. The general was pessimistic about China's ability to defend itself against Japan. When my father asked him outright, if he should send his family away, the general nodded his head gravely. Since Nanjing was the capital, it would most certainly be attacked.

The merchant had already left the city with his family. Baba only knew scribes, scholars and lowly civil servants, none of whom could get us out of the city. So he went to see Miss Rutherford, the only foreigner he knew. As it turned out, Miss Rutherford knew me because I had run some errands for her at Wu Jiao's suggestion. She was going to Hong Kong soon to sail home and agreed to take Mama and me, to pass us off as her servants. But Mama refused to leave. No amount of cajoling or even a rare display of anger on Baba's part could sway her.

In the middle of August, the first bombs fell on Nanjing. Baba stayed in the shop during the raids although he had helped the other merchants dig the bomb shelter under the back alleys. He was afraid the store would be looted. As the raids intensified and Mama became more frantic about his safety, Baba agreed to take cover if she allowed me to go to Hong Kong.

It was my turn to refuse to leave. I was sixteen and earning money. I was no longer a child. Baba insisted that I show him respect and Mama wouldn't go back on her word. When Miss Rutherford decided to take me to the train station herself, Baba didn't protest, afraid that she'd change her mind and leave without me. We said our goodbyes in the shop. Baba untied his leather apron and embraced me. Mama sobbed. Wu Jiao looked solemn.

The station was overrun with people trying to leave the city. The trains were packed: children squeezed into luggage racks, men climbing onto the roofs of the compartments while a few desperate young men strapped themselves under the carriage. Our train was delayed for hours. When I tried to leave at one point, Miss Rutherford grabbed my arm *and forced me to sit down. Your parents already gave you your life. The least you can do is save it.*

At breakfast, Helen slips her guidebook across the table. I take one look at the highlighted section and push it back. I am not interested in going to a museum dedicated to the Nanjing Massacre.

"It's as close to a grave as you will find."

How casually she says this. Her parents lie side by side in a cemetery which is maybe ten blocks from where they lived all their lives. She saw their coffins lowered into the ground, has had their names engraved on a headstone. The bones of my parents could be anywhere. In that construction pit on Taiping Lu, at the bottom of the Yangste River, or in any of the mass graves around the city. They probably weren't even together when they died.

And if my parents survived the invasion, they would have lost their home and their livelihood. They would have died as paupers and been buried in a common grave. Without anyone to ensure they were buried in the same one.

Memorial Hall of the Victims in Nanjing Massacre by Japanese Invaders. The godawful English translation, which I first noticed in the guidebook, is carved in stone at the entrance of the museum. Few museums are burdened with such a clumsy and accusatory marquee. Fewer still are built on a *wan ren keng*, a pit of ten thousand corpses, the site of a mass grave.

We wander through the Square of Mourning, the Square of Sacrifice, and look at the stones that represent other mass grave sites in and around Nanjing. Helen reads the English text on every stone while I focus on the shape and colour of the rock, the way the sun lights the edge of the copper plates on which the information has been inscribed. I pause in front of a granite wall in which figures of men have been carved, their hands tied behind their backs, their heads hanging down, walking towards their death. I don't linger but others stand transfixed, with tears in their eyes, my wife among them. As if feeling wretched can change what happened here or stop it from happening again.

We contemplate a large field of rubble with the statue of a fleeing woman and two tree stumps – a crude attempt at depicting the devastation of war. It looks so fake it makes me angry instead of desolate. Helen stares at the field for a long time, picks up a small chunk of pseudo-rubble and puts it in her jacket pocket.

We enter the exhibition hall which is half buried in the ground. *No picture taking. Solemn silence.* The signs are in English. Utilitarian, like you'd find on a construction site back home. There is a counter where visitors can buy candles and flowers.

A section of the mass grave is on display, behind glass, with little numbered cards tucked between the bones and skulls strewn there. In a museum, even bones are artifacts.

My wife buys me a sheaf of flowers and a candle for herself. She makes a sign of the cross and bows her head. She is not religious but she was raised a Catholic. She lights the candle and sets it down on the marble ledge and I lay the flowers beside it. I also bow my head but I don't know any prayers and even if I did, they would surely be inadequate.

Helen takes my arm as we enter the photo gallery. The first photographs we see were taken in Shanghai. Burning buildings, people running in the streets. Standard war shots. The next series shows the progress of the Japanese invaders as they march towards Nanjing, the damage they inflicted on Suzhou, Wuxi, Yangzhou, and Zhenjiang.

When we stand in front of the first photograph of Nanjing, Helen tightens her grip on my arm. It's a shot taken from the air on August 15, 1937, with three Japanese bombers in the foreground. August 1937! I was still living there then. I peer more closely but the picture is very grainy. The ink shop is in there somewhere, a collection of little grey dots. So is the market where Wu Jiao had his table and Miss Rutherford ran her dispensary.

Helen tugs at my sleeve. "Michael, people are lining up behind you."

August 15th. The day of the first bombardment. It was a Sunday. The air raid siren was going and I was watching the planes with Yuying and Zhao instead of going down to the shelter. We were more excited than scared.

"Please, dear. Move away from the picture. Let these people look at it."

When I step aside, three men, wearing red caps with China Tours printed on them, glance at the picture and frown at me. More people in red hats crowd behind them. I stumble forward and Helen reaches out to steady me.

I scan the walls on either side of us. I never realized there were so many photographs. Maybe, if I take the time to examine each one, I'll find my parents, I'll finally know what happened to them. It can't be worse than what I've already imagined.

So I move from one photograph to another. Jostle people out of my way. I skip over the pictures of dead children, of Chinese soldiers being rounded up, only looking for the faces of my mother and father. Scrutinize the lines of men being led to their deaths, searching for Baba's gaunt features and buck teeth. I find someone who looks like Wu Jiao. And another one. There seem to be many old men like Wu Jiao, with their old-fashioned clothes, thin beards, little caps.

But it's my parents I want to find. I look at every face, even the severed heads that are lined up against the wall, like turnips. I examine the face of every woman who is being raped, searching for Mama's. Shutting out the vulnerable, naked bodies. The way the women tried to cover their breasts and genitals with their hands.

You have to be methodical. You can't stop to take in what you're looking at otherwise you won't be able to go on. You have to be ruthless. Or you'll run out of time. Or you'll start to wail, like those women on the train, before they got too tired and hungry to panic at every sudden stop, every false alarm.

"Michael, please. You're scaring me."

Helen doesn't know the meaning of the word. I was so scared on that train I could taste my own shit. Not smell it. Taste it. Like it was coming up backwards. When I was beaten in the refugee camp, my heart thumped so hard my rib-cage was bruised inside as well as out.

Someone grabs my arm but it's not Helen. It's a security guard. He speaks to me quietly, asks me not to make a scene.

"A scene!" I shout in Mandarin. "Everyone here should be making a scene. Instead of staring in stunned silence. They should be wailing and falling to their knees ..."

People crowd around us and argue about what's wrong with me. There's no end to the speculation.

"Michael, listen to me."

I focus on Helen's face, on those steadfast blue eyes.

There's another man with us now. In a suit and tie. His face grim.

"He's all right now. Can't you see?" Helen begs. "He got upset because his parents died in the massacre."

I don't know if they died in the massacre, I want to cry out, but the words lodge in my throat. I don't know how they died. Did my father's head roll off his shoulders? Did my mother get dragged out into the street and raped?

The man leads us to a small office and pulls out chairs for us. Maybe this kind of meltdown is a common occurrence. They have their Square of Mourning, their Square of Sacrifice. What they need is a Square for Going Crazy with Grief. Going Crazy With Not Knowing. Going Crazy with Filial Regret. I should never have gone to Hong Kong. Emigrated to Canada. I should have stayed with my parents, shared their fate.

"I should never have brought you here," Helen mutters as she rubs my hands between hers, "I don't know what I was thinking."

I'm afraid to open my mouth. To moan out loud.

I remember what was on that scroll that Baba rolled up and slipped into my bag before I left the shop with Miss Rutherford. The one the bullies tore apart on my first day at the camp, dancing around me, hitting me with the two end pieces.

One step at a time is good walking.

I'll focus on that.

On placing one foot in front of the other.

Like a child who is learning to walk.

Like an old man who is afraid to fall.

fen	small coin
Lu	street
Sun Yat-sen	first president of China, died in 1925, buried in Nanjing in 1929
Yeye	paternal grandfather

MAL'ACHIM

At the bottom of the heart of every human being, from
earliest infancy until the tomb, there is something that
goes on indomitably expecting, in the teeth of all experience
of crimes committed, suffered and witnessed, that good
and not evil will be done to him. It is this above all that
is sacred in every human being.

SIMONE WEIL (D. 1943)

THE MOUNTAIN AIR IS PURE, with an edge to it, even in summer.

It feels like shattered glass.

I don't want to breathe this air but it flows through my lungs anyway. Invisible and omnipresent, like God. Leaving me to crave the dirty air of the city, the soot from the train station, the cigarette smoke and plaster dust in our apartment.

My nose indulges in each new smell. Woodsmoke. Pine and wildflowers. Mud and grass and manure. Smells that drift across the plateau without mingling.

I miss the noises of the city, the train station, the street. Before the Occupation muted them all. I miss the sounds of home. Maman at the piano, Papa tapping chisel against stone, my friends calling me from the courtyard.

There is so much silence here.

Thick and quilted like the cover on Maman's piano.

A silence that absorbs every noise.

That fills my ears with emptiness.

The boulanger is kind to me, the only person in the village who looks at me without suspicion. He is a big man with sloping shoulders, powerful arms and legs. The flour that clings to his skin and clothes is so coarse and grey he seems to be covered in ashes.

I am standing outside, at the end of the line, observing the boulanger through the window. I haven't sketched in my *calepin* since I left Paris and I hesitate to open it now, to slip the pencil out of the little loop on the side. *Wait*, Papa whispers. *Wait*. His voice faint and scratchy, as if I were hearing him on the radio. He never says much. A word. A sentence. And then he's gone.

Monsieur Gauthier lifts his head to greet the next customer, peering over glasses that are coated with flour. Like Papa used to peer at me, his glasses white with plaster dust. The same dust that clung to his skin and hair, seeped through his clothes, and poisoned his lungs.

I think Monsieur Gauthier was injured in the Great War. His right arm is stiffer than his left and he lists slightly to one side.

It was Papa who taught me how to study people. Not just their faces and bodies, but how they sit and stand and move. The way they hold a newspaper, a parcel, a handbag. Wear their hats, walk in their shoes. Who taught me to wait. To watch. To melt into the landscape, the park bench, the crowd. But that was in Paris. Here, in the village, it's not so simple. I am the stranger. The people stare at me, blatantly, like small children do. So I leave the *calepin* in my canvas bag. No point attracting more attention.

The line moves slowly. When I can finally step into the shop, I breathe in the flour, the sweet yeast, the burning embers in the oven, grateful that the coarser flour has only altered the taste of the bread and not its smell. There are no croissants here, no baguettes, forbidden as they are in Paris. Except on the black market the posters warn us about. Is there a black market here, in the villages of Quatre Montagnes?

I slide the ration cards and coupons across the counter, without a word. Monsieur Gauthier cuts the coupons he needs with the big black scissors that hang on a ribbon around his neck and returns the rest, leaving his floury prints on the cardboard. He winks as he hands me a *pain ordinaire*.

"Bonne journée, Mademoiselle." His voice is warm and moist, like his shop.

He doesn't mind that I don't speak, unlike the other shopkeepers who complain to Mademoiselle Moreau about my lack of manners. She tells them I'm *commotionnée*, shell-shocked, but it is a word reserved for soldiers and I have no right to it. No right at all.

I place the bread in the bicycle basket, on top of the potatoes and carrots and the dead rabbit. A stranger gave me the rabbit this morning just as I pedalled away from the farm. The man, who identified himself as François, stood so close to me I could smell the sweat on him. Traces of tobacco and freshly-cut wood. Motor oil.

I walk the *vélo* up the steep hill to the house which sits apart from the others on its own little lane. It looks different from the others too. Larger windows to let in the view, a recessed entrance with a small vestibule. The telescope in the window.

The telescope which caused such a fuss when we first arrived.

Mademoiselle had not been back to her father's house since his funeral. We spent the first day removing the sheets from the furniture, washing the dusty dishes, registering at the mairie. Buying provisions.

"My father was an amateur astronomer," Mademoiselle explained when she saw me standing by the telescope, "but the villagers thought he was a *fouineur*, a snoop. They considered him an outsider although his mother was born here and he spent all his summers in the village. Although he married a local girl and taught at the boys' school for forty years. But it wasn't the uncommon house he built that bothered them. Nor the large windows and the telescope. It was his stubborn, insatiable curiosity. The way he had to look at everything, touch everything, ask about everything."

She could've been describing my father. He too wanted to know everything, look at everything, touch everything.

"After my father died, I packed his books and clothes, but I didn't dismantle the telescope or roll up the constellation maps. Monsieur le Maire, whom my father despised, offered to buy the house. He coveted the larger windows, the prime location above the village, and was willing to pay a premium for it. I told him I'd rather burn it down than sell it to him."

An hour later, as if summoned by the recollection of that defiance, the mayor paid us a visit.

"Bonjour, Mademoiselle Moreau," he said, as he removed his hat.

His voice smelled of stomach acid and mineral water.

Mademoiselle, who was standing with her arms crossed, did not return his greeting.

"I am here to inform you that you have to dismantle your telescope and bring it to the mairie. If you have a radio or binoculars, you must turn them in as well. War time regulations, you understand."

"The war is over. We lost," Mademoiselle reminded him as she closed the inner door in his face, leaving him to fume in the vestibule (which he may have also coveted).

So now we are known as *les espionnes*. We just haven't figured out who we are spying for, the Vichy government or the English.

Mademoiselle is playing the piano when I reach the house and doesn't hear me enter. It's so badly out of tune she only plays when I'm out. She has contacted the only *accordeur* in Quatre Montagnes but has not been able to arrange his transportation from Villard de Lans. There is a shortage of petrol and those who travel the nine kilometres by horse and wagon are too busy ferrying people to the doctor, the dentist or the bedside of ailing relatives, to offer a place to a piano tuner. Even if he is blind and a veteran of the last war.

She stops when she realizes I'm standing there. Smiles when I hold up the rabbit. "I only play to keep my fingers moving," she explains in a gentle voice, so unlike the sharp, aggrieved tones she used in her classroom.

Whenever I'm alone in the house, I sit at the piano and practise my scales with the lid down, my fingers eager to dance on any surface, even a silent one. If Mademoiselle stays away long enough, I pretend to play some Chopin or Schumann, or my own compositions. Rewriting and rearranging them in my mind.

Mademoiselle stashes her music book in the bench.

"My grandmother taught piano in Grenoble," she explains, "And after she died, my father was determined to bring her piano up here. The fool he hired didn't tie it to the trailer properly and it fell out before it reached the village. It crashed into the valley, narrowly missing some hikers and killing a cow that was grazing. Undeterred, my father paid the farmer for his cow, found another piano, and another fool to bring it up."

I imagine the rope breaking, the piano slamming against the side of the trailer and toppling out. The long fall into the valley below. The hikers scurrying out of the way, three, maybe four of them, the hapless cow. The piano lying in pieces, the keys dangling from snapped hammer shanks.

Maman wouldn't be able to imagine it – her heart would break and splinter in the process. We once found a violin that someone had thrown out of a window. The violin was badly damaged but she brought it to Monsieur Ducellier anyway, to his tiny shop on rue Maine. He took one look at it and laughed, comparing her to a child bringing a dead bird to her father and expecting him to make it fly again.

I look down, half expecting to find a dead bird instead of a rabbit.

"You are allowed to miss her," Mademoiselle says as she removes the stiff little body from my hand.

How did she know I was thinking about my mother?

By the time I follow her outside, she has already peeled the fur off the rabbit and stretched it on a makeshift frame. I'm sure she'll find a use for it – she never lets anything go to waste. If the girls at the lycée could see her now, skinning rabbits, chopping wood, building a chicken coop, their scorn would wither in their throats.

She hands me the pail and I fetch water from the cistern, a wooden pail that is almost impossible to carry when it's full. The metal pails that were collected for scrap at the start of the war are rusting in a pile with other metal objects beside the boys' school. I let the handle dig deep into my hand, the weight yank on muscle and bone. The pain more real than I am.

Mademoiselle has already carved up the animal when I return and is browning the meat in the frying pan, the heavy one I can hardly lift off its nail on the wall.

I scrub the potatoes and the carrots outside, the water from the bucket icy against my hands. The smell of the meat assails my nose anyway. When I finish scrubbing the vegetables, I seek refuge under the trees at the back of the house. I breathe in the pine needles, the sap, the bark, but all I can smell is the dead rabbit.

The piano, a beautiful Pleyel, was too big for the room. It didn't belong to us — it had been abandoned by the previous tenant, a concert pianist who had fallen on hard times. Maman kept it covered to protect it from Papa's plaster dust.

I crawled under the piano and folded back the quilted cover so the light from the window could reach me. I opened my new cahier. All my notebooks were rejects, their covers torn or missing, deemed unsaleable by the papeterie at the corner where Maman worked two mornings a week. One of the many jobs she juggled to make ends meet.

I could smell the beeswax Maman used to polish the piano, the starch of my school uniform, the shavings of the pencil I had just sharpened.

The words I had collected that day were dancing in my head and I was eager to write them down:

> *églantine: a wild rose, a soft and elegant word, without thorns*
>
> *verroterie: coloured glass to make jewellery, to trap the light against the skin*
>
> *affrettando: quick, hurried; the way Liszt should be played; the way Papa talks*
>
> *cartomancie: reading the future in a deck of cards, a gamble of a different kind*

What are you doing under there, Papa demanded before I had a chance to write the last word. I scrambled out, the matelassé slipping off the piano and pooling at his feet. You should be playing the piano, Madeleine, not hiding under it. Finishing that sketch you started on Sunday, instead of wasting your time scribbling.

Yes, Papa, I answered, gathering the cover and draping it over the piano, tugging it here and there to make it hang just right. Hoping he wouldn't ask to see what I'd been writing.

Papa was looking for his cigarettes now. I retreated to my room and wrote down the last word, my best find:

palimpseste: writing which has been erased, written over, but still haunts the page.

I hear the truck first, as it struggles up the hill. Smell the wood-smoke. When someone raps on the door, my first instinct is to hide, although Mademoiselle has told me not to. What if it's the mayor again? Or someone who wants to take me away?

There is another sharp rap. "Simone, it's François. I have a surprise for you."

François. The man who gave us the rabbit. I open the door, hoping for a chicken, only to find a man with a scarred face and a toolbox. François has already climbed into the truck which has a strange contraption on it, the source of the woodsmoke. I stare at the piano tuner. The ravaged nose, the twisted mouth, the unseeing eyes. When I don't speak up, the man extends his hand, not quite in my direction.

"Mademoiselle? I am Pierre Faure. I've come to tune the piano."

I have to step down and sideways to shake his outstretched hand. He feels his way up my arm with his other hand and clamps it above my elbow.

"This way, Monsieur," I force myself to speak, the words thick and dry on my tongue, like a bundle of herbs.

I guide him but he seems to know the place. He's not surprised by the inner door and when we step inside, he turns to the left, feeling his way to the piano. What else does this man do? How many pianos could there be up here, in the villages of Quatre Montagnes?

As he runs his hands over the keys, he winces at the sound, which makes the scars around his eyes contract and give him an even more hideous look.

"Did Simone tell you the story of her grandmother's piano, the one that crashed into the valley?"

"Yes."

"Well, I learned to play on that piano. May it rest in peace. And it was Simone's grandmother who suggested I become a piano tuner after I came home blind from the war. She recommended me to the parents of her students and since she was the best music teacher in Grenoble, this included people who could afford to pay."

He is difficult to understand, his words distorted by the scarring around his mouth. He continues to talk as he unlatches his box and sets out his tools on a blue cloth, as he struggles to remove the front panel of the piano. It is only when he starts to adjust the pins that he falls silent.

I pull out my calepin and slide the pencil out of the loop. No need to wait, to blend into the overstuffed chair – he cannot see me. I sketch him quickly. The man's face is a surrealist's dream: the skin tight across the cheekbones, loose around the eyes, the scar tissue pink against the brown and leathery face.

Surrealists don't have dreams, Papa scoffs, *only nightmares.*

"Who else is here?" Monsieur Faure asks.

How could he hear Papa's voice inside my head?

"I thought I felt someone. Must have been an air current or something. You would not believe how distracting it is to be blind. It's as if every noise and smell and texture in the universe wants your attention."

He is an *anomalie* like me. A freak.

I close the calepin, slip the pencil back in the loop. It's the kind of calepin Papa always carried with him, about the size of an identity card, with a cream cloth cover which I have festooned with ink drawings. He gave it to me on my last birthday – there was no money for a present – from the meagre supply he kept in his bottom drawer.

I watch Monsieur Faure as he tightens each pin and my body responds to every adjustment he makes, as if he were tuning me, equalizing my temperament.

When Mademoiselle comes home, she rushes over to the man with a cry of delight. Kisses the heavily scarred cheeks. "Pierre, I can't believe you're finally here!"

I have never seen Mademoiselle so light on her feet, so intimate in her greeting. She drags him away from the piano and makes him sit in the chair I've just vacated. She hurries off to the kitchen and returns with a dusty bottle and three glasses.

"It's my last bottle of cider."

I sit sideways on the bench that runs under the large picture window so I can glance outside from time to time. When Mademoiselle brings me a glass, I lift it to my nose and sniff the fermented apples. The smell reminds me of Katou who brought us two bottles of cider every time she returned from Bretagne.

"How long can you stay?" she asks Monsieur Faure, as she sits on the arm of his chair, her hand on his shoulder.

"Only until four. François showed up at the door this morning with a wood-burning contraption on his truck. I barely had time to get my tools together."

I can understand him better now. It's like adjusting to a thick accent.

"So the whole town must've seen you arrive."

"It's better that way. The more openly we travel the less people will think anything is going on."

"Like the war?"

"The war is over. We lost. As you yourself told the mayor."

They laugh at this, heartily, their heads almost touching. I fail to see the humour in it. I didn't like the way the mayor looked at me that day, the way his eyes narrowed in his pudgy face.

I could smell everyone's supper as I followed Papa down the stairs: Madame Garnier's cassoulet, Madame Tessier's rabbit stew, Monsieur Martin's burnt sausages. Madame la concierge was standing in the doorway, trying to escape the stink of her husband's cigar or the back of his hand, if he was already drinking. She gave us a sad, distracted smile, which Papa didn't notice, his eyes already on the street.

We went for a walk every evening. I would've liked to walk more quickly or at least more steadily but Papa stopped so often I had to slow down or stop at the next corner to wait for him. I used this time to compose little melodies that I jotted down in the calepin I kept in the pocket of my dress .

As I rounded the first corner, I inhaled the soap and bleach from the lavoir public. The scummy water. The whiff of rust from the clotheslines. Papa was already trailing behind me, his hands in his pockets, his eyes darting from one side of the street to the other. He stopped to look at the dusty frames in Monsieur Didier's window, to chat with Monsieur Lambert about the cost of paint. Papa was a sculptor and a painter but earned his living as a plasterer. Not that anyone was hiring in those hard times.

Papa's hands never stayed in his pockets for long. He had to touch everything, no matter how familiar. The stuccoed walls, the corrugated shutters, the wrought iron detailing on the windows and doors. I imagined him as a boy, pressing his face in every shop window, petting every dog he met, dragging a stick on the cobblestones.

The sky was the colour of smudged ink by the time we reached rue Émile Richard, which cut through the cemetery. It was my favourite street, lined with trees and souls instead of buildings, the only street in Paris without numbers, according to Papa. Even there he tarried, running his hands over the bark of the plane trees because their branches — bursting with new leaves — were beyond his reach.

Boulevard Raspail marked the end of the street, the quiet of the cemetery. Its sidewalks were crowded, the traffic heavy, but Papa walked at the same pace, oblivious to the impatience of those who jostled us, who turned around to glare at us. When we entered the café-tabac at the corner of rue Campagne Première, Monsieur Henri had already filled a pichet with red wine for Papa and poured a citron pressé for me.

I took my usual place at the window where I could watch the passers-by. Sipping my drink, my nose giddy with lemons. Papa stood at the bar to drink and smoke and sketch while he listened to Monsieur Henri's litany of woes. It was a lively litany, filled with wit and humour rather than despair.

Later, as we walked home, Papa asked me what had caught my attention that evening. He always asked me this so I knew to have an answer ready. I told him about the red crinoline I had seen sticking out of a garbage can, the playing card, a seven of spades, someone had taped to a window, the young boy struggling to unload bags of sand off a truck.

I didn't see the crinoline nor the seven of spades, he said. The boy I noticed. A country boy dizzy with everything he's seen since arriving in the city.

Mademoiselle has not spoken since Pierre Faure left two days ago. She has not turned on the radio nor touched the piano. I don't understand her silence which I find more oppressive, more unnerving than my own. We're sitting by the large picture window, unravelling her father's old sweaters and rewinding the wool.

I wonder if the villagers can see us, if we look like mannequins in a department store window.

What could Monsieur Faure have said or done to upset her so? They seemed so happy to have found each other again.

Mademoiselle Moreau has a sour face that must have been pretty once, eyes the colour of pale blue glass, brown hair that she wears in a thick braid down her back. Her body is angular and thin, her bosom flat. The students at the lycée used to call her La Morose, because she was always so glum. The more cruel ones called her La Morue, the Cod.

"Did Monsieur Faure say when he would be back?"

Her face doesn't register surprise although I've barely spoken since we arrived in the village. I have been so *engourdie*, so numb.

"What happened to him?" I persist, "in the war?"

She is tugging at the stitches of an ugly green sweater. Her eyes are opaque now, not like glass at all. Her skin as grey as Monsieur Gauthier's war-time flour. Her voice, when she finally speaks, is altered too, dull and listless.

"He was supposed to be safe. They were both supposed to be safe. They were stretcher bearers, not soldiers. They had just brought in their last casualty when the field hospital was hit by a shell. Pierre survived, his brother didn't."

The half-unravelled sweater slips off her lap and falls to the floor. "They weren't just brothers but twins and so close that people called them Jean-Pierre, as if they were one person."

Which one of them had she loved? Jean or Pierre? The one who was killed or the one who came home blind and brotherless?

I continue to unravel the sweater on my lap, pulling on the coarse grey wool without rewinding it, until I have a tangled mess on my hands.

I drag my suitcase out from under the bed and take the first cahier I find there. I pick a page at random and read the five words I wrote that day, May 28, 1939, more than three years ago now, in what seems like another lifetime:

> *escamoter*: to conjure away; make a card disappear, a coin, the truth about our family
>
> *écho*: repetition, reverberation, rumour, a second chance
>
> *seuil*: sill, doorstep, entrance, transition; the way into a house, a room, a soul
>
> *naguère*: recently, not long ago, before our memory rearranged it all
>
> *zigzag*: a broken line, the shape of the letter z, the way some music folds back on itself

Sometimes I scan the sky for one of the constellations outlined on Monsieur Moreau's maps even though I am hopeless at it. Patterns have always eluded me. Maps have never made sense. When Mademoiselle takes pity on me and aligns the telescope with the constellation I am seeking, I squint into the eyepiece and pretend that I can make it out.

I only touch the telescope because it reminds me of Papa. Because he used to take me to l'Observatoire, just a few blocks from our apartment, on the first Saturday of the month, and one night a year, when its doors were open to the public. He didn't know much about stars but he loved to walk through the exhibits, to run his hands over the instruments on display until the watchman chased him away. L'Observatoire is closed now and a large Nazi flag obscures the upper window above the main entrance.

Papa waited until I was seven to take me to see the sculpture I had been named after. Seven, the age of reason, the age of my First

Communion, when I thought I was pure and white like an angel. The same year Loïc spat on me in the courtyard and called me une sale petite juive, a dirty little Jewess.

When Papa brought me to the Louvre that day, I still didn't know I was Jewish, that I should never have been named after a work of art or a Catholic saint. Of course, Papa would argue that Marie-Madeleine was Jewish before she was a saint or a work of art.

I was afraid to look at the Erhart statue, to discover that it was not as beautiful as the drawings that hung in my bedroom. I need not have worried. My father's drawings, as fine as they were, could not capture the beauty that loomed over us. I recognized the half-closed eyes, the delicate nose, the wide forehead, the long wavy hair but now they were real. So real the head seemed about to turn, the eyes to widen, the arms to open in embrace.

We admired her together, in silence, hand in hand. When it was time to leave, he lifted me and let me touch the wooden contour of the saint's face, the strands of her hair, her delicate hands. Even though it wasn't allowed.

A sculpture had to be touched to be appreciated.

I first encounter the boy on the road that leads to the farm where I buy our vegetables. He doesn't look up as I pedal past him. He's wearing city clothes that are too small for him, that no boy from around here would wear. The next time I see him he's sprawled under my favourite tree, a giant spruce, on the outskirts of the village.

"Bonjour," he greets me as he scrambles to his feet.

I can't tell if he was waiting for me or just happened on the spot himself. I'm so used to not speaking that I don't open my mouth even though I want to.

"You're the girl who doesn't speak. Madame Grissot told me about you. My name is Julien."

He says this without hesitation but I feel it anyway. Julien is not his real name. I shake his outstretched hand.

"I'm from Paris," he continues. "The 16th district. What about you?"

Maman had many piano students in that neighbourhood. I used to accompany her there and I remember the beautiful houses, the tree-lined streets. This boy could have been one of her students; our paths could have already crossed.

"Can you sit with me? You don't have to speak if you don't want to."

When I take the calepin out of my pocket and wave my pencil around, he nods eagerly. I sit on the ground and wait for him to settle. Taking in his large brown eyes, his badly cut hair.

"You're going to write down your answers?" he asks, misunderstanding the purpose of the calepin. I shake my head and pretend to sketch in the air.

He smiles broadly, revealing big square teeth. Strikes an exaggerated pose, which he abandons instantly. I flip to a fresh page, start to draw his face. He turns his head so often I leave the face unfinished and concentrate on the rest of him.

"Are you Jewish?" he asks. Too curious to stay quiet for long.

As I sketch his jacket, I imagine a yellow star on the brown tweed. I take my time with the sketch, gathering as much detail as possible, returning to his face now that he isn't moving around so much. He chatters at me, like Monsieur Faure did. It seems that the more silent I become, the more people around me need to talk.

I didn't collect five words a day at the beginning, just the ones I happen to notice, maybe a dozen a week. I remember the first three words I recorded: *appassionatamente*, with passion, my favourite direction in music; *maillet,* because Papa was trying out the new mallet he had just bought; and *cerfeuil,* an herb Katou liked to use in her cooking.

I can avoid the large spruce at the outskirts of the village but there is only one road to the Bartoli farm and Julien lies in wait for me not far from the farm gate, on the very spot where François handed me the rabbit. I can taste that rabbit just thinking about it.

"Don't be afraid," he pleads as he approaches. "I just want to be your friend."

My friend. In Paris we never would've moved in the same circles. He wouldn't have given me a second glance or spoken to me. When I entered a house in his neighbourhood, I had to stay in the kitchen while Maman taught her lesson.

I have one foot on the pedal, the other foot on the ground. Worried that someone will see us together.

"I will wait for you here."

I cycle down the lane. The farmer is waiting for me at the next gate, his smile trapped under a bushy black mustache. He holds up three small tomatoes.

"Just for you, signorina. Please don't show them to anyone. I want no trouble from the mayor. I told him I couldn't grow tomatoes up here in the mountains."

The tomatoes are still warm from the sun, their leaves giving off a sharp, smoky smell. I haven't eaten a tomato in more than two years. Monsieur Bartoli fills the basket with a large cabbage, three onions and a turnip while I nestle the tomatoes in my canvas bag so they will not get crushed.

I pay him in Italian liras and not francs. I have no idea where Mademoiselle gets the liras or why the farmer wants them. Maybe he has family in Italy and needs to send them money.

"Be careful with that boy," he says as I swing my leg over the bicycle.

Because he's a boy or because he's a Jew?

Julien is still leaning against the first gate. He gives me a shy smile and we walk together towards the village. He does all the talking and I shake my head, shrug, or smile. He drops back when we reach the outskirts.

I was lying under the piano with the letter Madame la concierge had given me. A letter from Maman's sister in Canada. There was a photograph inside, I could feel the edges of it through the envelope. I wanted to rip the letter open and read it before Maman came home, but I didn't dare. Maman was very particular about her sister's letters. It was perhaps the only sister she had. I didn't know my mother's family nor my father's. We are your family, my father would answer impatiently if I asked. My parents have disowned me, Maman would reply, without ever telling me why.

My parents argued about the letter later, as I knew they would. Maman wanted us to move to Canada before another war broke out, another grande guerre like the one I was studying at school. She was worried about what was happening to the Jews in Germany.

We have nothing to worry about, Papa argued. We're French citizens. As were our parents and grandparents. Why do you think so many Jews are flocking to France? Because they know they will be safe here. And your sister was only allowed into Canada because she lied on her application. They don't want Jews there either.

The next day, Maman read me her sister's letter and showed me the picture of my cousin Solange, who looked a lot like me. I asked her why she wanted us to move so far away.

Because we'll be safer there.

We are not safe here?
When you're Jewish, you're never safe.

"What do you miss most about Paris?" Julien asks, the next time we walk together.

His voice is sticky and sweet like caramel. His eyes are the colour of Maman's old leather satchel. He plays the violin – I can tell from the calluses on his long, delicate fingers.

"I miss the way it smells."

He stares at me. It's the first time I've spoken to him.

The way it smells? Papa asks.

I've started to collect words again and record them on the back cover of my *calepin* in my tiniest script. I reread them often, like a miser caressing his gold coins.

> *lauzes*: thin, flat stones found on roof gables and along
> the roads here, solid, immutable
> *trimballer*: to lug around or drag behind a heavy box, a
> suitcase, a lifetime of regret
> *citerne*: a water tank, carved out of stone, like the bottom
> of my soul
> *châler*: a local expression, to ride behind someone on a
> bicycle, like a stowaway
> *stellaire des bois*: a delicate flower with thin white petals
> that look like fairies dancing

The colours are different here, just like the smells. Purer, clearer. The blues are particularly striking, perhaps because the sky is so vast it dims the rest of the spectrum. There is a blue haze over everything. Even my dreams are tinged with blue.

I sit under a pine behind the house and conjure up all the blues I can remember. The dark blue dress that Maman wore to play the piano at the Café Versailles, the lovely satin folds, the sound of the crinoline underneath, like butterfly wings rubbing together. The *sarrau* Papa wore to plaster houses, to work at his sculpture. Katou's eyes. The alcove off the kitchen, which served as my bedroom, its one tiny window overlooking the courtyard, its walls a faded blue. Packages of cigarettes, Gitanes for Maman, Gauloises for Papa. Picasso's blue period.

The blue-mauve of Monet's lily ponds

That blue velvet dress Madame Picard made for your first concert, adds Papa.

As soon as Katou disrobed, I knew why Papa had asked the young woman to model for him. She was the embodiment of the Sainte Marie-Madeleine statue my father so admired, the one I had been named after. The narrow shoulders, the small breasts, the long hair, thick and tangled like a mermaid. She was so nervous she tried to hide her breasts with her hair which only made her look more like the Erhart statue.

She worked at a crêperie on rue des Rennes and had decided to supplement her meagre salary by posing for artists, not realizing they were poorer than she was.

Katou's eyes were a watery blue, like the sea she had left behind. I sketched her with sand under her feet and seashells in her hair.

"What smells do you miss?" Julien wants to know when he sees me again.

"All of them."

"Name me one."

How can I name just one, when there are so many?

"The way the cobblestones smelled when it rained," I offer before I pedal away.

"Marie-Madeleine, come back..."

How does he know my name?

"What other smells do you miss?" Julien shouts at me two days later as I pass him on the way to the farm. He is still waiting when I cycle back with a basket full of *courgettes*. Steps in front of me to force me to slow down.

He stands over the front wheel, his hands on the handlebars. "Another smell."

"Lavender."

"What kind of lavender? Freshly-cut? Dried? In your mother's cologne?"

"In pots on Madame Garnier's balcony."

"Who is Madame Garnier? Your concierge?"

I push the bicycle forward, forcing him to step back, to release the handlebars. As I speed away, the bicycle rolls over a *lauze* that has toppled on the road and I lose my balance.

"The smell of real coffee. Real bread. Fish and oysters and mussels."

We are lying on our backs, in a field, surrounded by fragrant wildflowers, most of which we cannot name. Obsessing about the smells of food we cannot have. That we haven't had since the beginning of the Occupation.

"What else?" Julien demands. He is like a child, always wanting more.

"Strawberries. Every June, Papa would take me to Les Halles very early and we would wander through the rows of baskets, the thousands of baskets on the cobblestones. Intoxicated by the smell of so many berries, our eyes seared by too much red."

Katou was not the only woman who posed for my father, although she was his favourite. Her face was plain but her ass magnificent, Papa and his friends were fond of saying. They raved about the line of her back, the length of her legs, the curve of her breasts, like she was a geometry assignment.

The other women who posed for my father were older but I found their bodies more interesting, more inspiring. For I was allowed to sketch them too, as long as I stayed in my corner and kept quiet. A strange admonition given I was always quiet and Papa was the one who was noisy, explosive, in perpetual motion.

Madame Picard ran the blanchisserie on rue Daguerre. She was hunched from years of bending over other people's dirty clothes, her hands red and flaky from the harsh soap she used. She had small breasts, good legs, a sagging belly. Wore expensive dresses of the finest wool, in beautiful dark colours like burgundy and purple, which she carefully draped over a chair when she disrobed. Had she made them herself or had someone, a sister perhaps, given them to her? She was the one who made my first recital dress from a pair of blue velvet drapes.

Madame Giraud was as fat and pink as the hams that hung at the back of her husband's charcuterie. Her hair thick and dark, her eyes full of mischief. She loved to gossip, to sing, to laugh, and to eat.

Madame Voronova was Russian. She had been a beauty in her day, you could tell from the way she held her head, as if offering it to be admired. In the contours of her cheekbones, now smeared with too much rouge. She didn't disrobe, just unbuttoned her dress to reveal her cleavage. She always wore the same black dress, the same shawl with the gaudy embroidered roses. I loved to draw her face, her wrinkles, her dark eyes, as large and unblinking as a deer's.

The body I knew best was my mother's. She was as small and lithe as Katou, although she was twenty years older. Her breasts soft and round, her nipples the colour of the rose draperies in the salon, her derrière high and firm.

I never saw my mother naked, Maman volunteered once, as she stepped out of the black dress she wore to play the piano in fancy restaurants. The one she alternated with the blue satin. I fingered the velvet, soft and limp like the petals of a flower past its prime, eager to hear more about my grandmother but Maman was leaning out the window, listening to a street singer.

"What is your real name?"

"Samuel. And yours?"

"Marie-Madeleine is my real name. I've been baptized and I've made my First Communion. I didn't even know I was Jewish until I was seven years old."

"So, your parents are assimilated."

Assimilated? We are atheists and communists! Papa shouts in my ear.

"My parents lived their lives free from religion."

"So why did they have you baptized? Have you take your First Communion?"

"To protect me."

"What about God's protection?"

"I don't think He's doing much to protect Jews. Do you?"

These were the words that caught my attention on July 11, 1940:
  caminando: gentle progression in music; the way Papa
    meanders on our evening walks
  attiser: to stoke a fire, a quarrel, a masterpiece from a pile of stone

siroter: to sip; to drink slowly; to suck the marrow
out of each new word

sussurer: to whisper, to soothe, to maintain an
illusion of safety

élixir: a magic potion, a liquid transformation

Monsieur Gauthier is kind to all his customers, even those who claim he sells whiter bread on the side. He greets each one with the same warmth, asks after the family, offers support to those whose sons or husbands are prisoners of war, in forced labour in Germany, or in hiding. I work on my sketch as I wait in line. He gave me permission to draw his likeness last week, neither of us uttering a word.

The woman behind me peers over my shoulder. I can feel her breath on my neck, hear her tell her companion: "See how she draws? Like her grandfather did. And her uncles."

What is she talking about?

I hear something else the next day when I line up at the mairie for the September ration coupons. The wait is long and the stares make it seem interminable.

"She looks just like her." There is tittering as the comment travels down the line.

The mayor's wife examines our identity cards, her bulging eyes shifting from Mademoiselle's picture to mine. She stamps our ration cards and hands me the new coupon sheets. I try to imagine her and her husband living in the Moreau house but I can't. They don't deserve to live there, their minds too narrow for those beautiful picture windows.

When I reach the house, Mademoiselle is unpacking boxes. She slides one across to me and I kneel on the stone floor to rummage through it. There are sketch pads, a box of Baignol and Farjon pencils, sticks of charcoal, a tin of watercolours. All unused.

"They belonged to my father. You're welcome to use them."

I take the familiar pencil box and pull out the tray. Finger the six red and gold pencils without taking one. Papa loved these pencils but had to settle for the ones Maman could get at a discount at the papeterie.

"The people in the village think you're my mother," I tell her as we eat our supper. She shrugs as she dips the crumbly bread into the cabbage soup. "It doesn't surprise me. They don't have much imagination. I return with a girl who's young enough to be my daughter so they figure that's why I stayed away all those years."

"But I don't look like you at all."

"It doesn't matter. You are slim, your hair is the same colour as mine. My father and brothers loved to draw. They're just bolstering the conclusions they've already reached."

So she has brothers. Why does she never mention them?

"As long as they think you're my daughter, they won't speculate about you being Jewish and this makes it safer for you."

I was still awake. I could hear Katou breathing, smell the sea and sand in her hair. Katou had spent the summer with her family in Bretagne and had returned that afternoon, her skin glowing from the sun, her eyes a restless blue, her pockets full of shells for me. She had met a new man, an Englishman, and she taught me a few English words, including seashell.

Katou often stayed with us, sometimes for weeks at a time. She was always looking for a new room, a new roommate, a new lover. She would often cook for us: crepes filled with mushrooms, oeufs à la bretonne, or her delicious fish stew. Usually she slept on blankets on the floor because my bed was too narrow but that night she had climbed in with me, had fallen asleep instantly, her back against the wall, her arms around my waist.

I smelled his peppermint pastille before I heard Papa's step in the corridor. He often wandered through the apartment when he couldn't sleep. By the time he entered the alcove that served as my bedroom, I could hear him wheeze.

Katou, he whispered. Where are you? Rummaging through the blankets, surprised not to find her there.

I waited till he was gone to slip out of bed, to crawl under the blankets on the floor so Katou would not hear me weep.

My arms ache. My nose is happy with the smell of freshly-cut wood. Mademoiselle pulls the blade towards her and I struggle to pull it back. We are sawing the trees that François cut down for us, from the small woodlot granted to us by the village. The winter will be harsh up here and much longer than in Paris so we have to prepare for it.

"Do your brothers live in Grenoble? Or Marseille?" I ask, figuring they didn't live up here, in Quatre Montagnes, or they would have visited.

"They both died at Verdun."

I wait for her to say more but she doesn't. Her eyes as opaque as the day she told me what happened to Jean and Pierre Faure.

Later, I find her brothers' names on the war memorial near the church.

Charles et Louis Moreau, 1916. And just above, Jean Faure, 1917.

No wonder we found her so morose.

"What was your favourite place?"
"The train station."

I lean against the spruce until I can feel the bark through the cotton of my dress. Close my eyes. I don't know why I said the train station when it was Papa's favourite place, not mine. He loved to sit on the bench facing the ticket counters and draw the people waiting in line. If he didn't have his calepin, he sketched on whatever he could find, the margins of a newspaper or a timetable, brown wrapping paper, a laundry ticket. There were scraps of paper all over the apartment, littering the table in the front hall, the piano cover, the windowsills.

"What did you like about it? The idea of going somewhere else? The crowd? Lovers being reunited?"

"No. It was the movement, the noise, the smell of the railroad tracks."

He laughed. "And what do railroad tracks smell like?"

"Wet wood and gravel. Tar. Soot. Pigeon shit."

I like the way he laughs with his whole body.

Why don't you ever mention your parents, ma petite Mado? Papa asks.

Don't call me your petite Mado.

We're out of breath from the climb. We can't see the valley below as the clouds have swarmed over the ridge, trapping us in their wet embrace. It is disconcerting, like being lost in a fog.

We lie down on our blanket and let the whiteness swirl over us.

Julien leans over to kiss me.

Loïc kissed me on the lips when I was wearing my First Communion dress. He kissed me many times over the summer, calling me sa belle petite juive. I didn't know what it meant. Thought it was an endearment of some kind. We were both seven. Then one day he spat at me, and I became a dirty little Jewess instead of a beautiful one.

Pierre Faure returns to work on the piano. He's alone in the house, his tools scattered around him, when I return after climbing with Julien.

"I let myself in," he explains, when he hears me enter.

I remove Mademoiselle's boots. They're too big for me so I have to wear several pairs of socks to keep them on my feet.

"I know I should never have kissed you—"

"Monsieur Faure, it's me. Marie-Madeleine."

He turns his head in the direction of my voice. Smiles. At this angle and with his hair falling over his face, he looks normal. I don't know why but the thought of him kissing Mademoiselle thrills me.

"So you were hiking?"

"Yes."

"Did you take that boy with you?"

"What boy?"

"The young man from Lyon. The one François brought here."

Strange that Julien has never mentioned François. Or that he came here from Lyon instead of Paris.

Monsieur Faure is already packing his tools so he must've been here a while.

"I think the piano is much improved. It will probably need one more adjustment. I don't suppose I could persuade you to play for me?"

When I don't respond, he shrugs. "Maybe next time."

I carry his tool box outside and wait with him.

François arrives in his wood-fuelled truck. As he takes the tool box from me and places it in the back, I wonder if Julien was hiding under the tarp there when he was first brought here. I watch as the truck drives down the hill, across the square, and onto the road to Villard de Lans.

"Tell me about another favourite place."

"Tell me one of yours."

"The candy shop I went to every Saturday, after my violin lesson."

"And what did you buy?"

"I would look over every tray but I always ordered pralines, two or three, depending how many coins I had in my pocket. What is your favourite candy?"

"Caramels."

"I thought so."

"Why?"

"Because it takes a long time to work your way to the centre, to break it down, to release its sweetness."

"What else do you miss?" This is how Julien always greets me.

If I ask him what he misses, he talks about his best friend Rémi, his lycée, his violin teacher. I asked him about Lyon once but he became so agitated I have not mentioned it since.

"So what else do you miss?"

"The noise."

"What kind of noise?"

I have to laugh. At his persistence, his doggedness.

"The traffic on the boulevards. The cars honking. The trains roaring into Gare Montparnasse. The métropolitain rumbling under my feet. Crowds of people everywhere, talking and laughing. Before the Occupation."

anicroche: a snag, a hitch, but in times like these, a catastrophe

chiaroscuro: light-dark, contrast, when darkness gives shape to light

bagatelle: a trifle, a whimsical composition,
what a life is worth
anéantir: annihilate, reduce to nothing; such a soft
and delicate word for such a harsh deed
mitzvah: a commandment, a religious obligation,
a good deed, a lot of weight for one word

The concert was at seven and we still hadn't reached the metro station. We would have to stand at the back of the church as the concert was free and Madeleine de Valmalète well known. Maman had studied with her at the Conservatoire. Had been following her career for years, clipping articles, collecting programmes from friends who could afford tickets to her concerts. Madame de Valmalète had given Maman two of her recordings but we had no gramophone on which to play them. Madame Garnier would let us listen to the recordings but only if I walked her arthritic dog.

Maman was rummaging in her bag for a coin to give to the flute player at the corner of rue de Chevreuse. She had stopped to listen to him although we were in a rush, although the man played there every day.

We hurried down the next block. My mother took me to concerts all over the city, free ones as we had no money for tickets, but we were invariably late. Maman was worse than Papa for stopping and starting. Any sound would distract her. A church bell, a bird singing, rain running off the roof of a kiosk. The musicians at every corner, the street singers.

There was a woman singing near the metro station. Her feet were bare, her dress dirty, her hair as long and tangled as Katou's. I tried to steer Maman away but she had already slowed down to listen.

The woman had a beautiful voice, polished, trained, not the raw voice of a street singer.

Maman waited for her to finish her song but didn't open her purse for another coin. When the small crowd dispersed, she helped the woman gather the coins that had been thrown at her feet. I helped too, anxious for us to get away.

Hannah, it's me. Myriam. Come, I'll buy you some food.

Myriam? Why was she calling herself Myriam when her name was Marianne?

The three of us went into the nearest café and Maman ordered an omelette and a coffee for the woman who had yet to utter a word.

I was still hoping we'd get to the concert. The Mozart sonata I wanted to hear was at the end of the programme and Maman had promised to introduce me to the pianist afterwards. She was the Madeleine I had been named after, according to Maman, and not the Erhart statue.

The woman ate the omelette quickly and all the bread.

Hannah, what has happened to you? Why are you singing in the streets?

The woman didn't answer.

We never went to the concert and I never met Madeleine de Valmalète. Maman insisted the woman come home with us. She slept in Maman's bed and Papa was relegated to the floor of my room, where he kept me awake with his snoring. Hannah disappeared the next day and Maman cried for a week without ever telling me who she was.

I trip over Monsieur Faure's tool box in the vestibule. I rush into the house but there is no sign of him or Mademoiselle, although there is a cabbage half chopped on the kitchen table. As I climb the stairs to the second storey, I hear them laughing. I know they are naked because people laugh differently without their clothes on. Mademoiselle has clearly forgiven him for kissing her.

So I sneak back downstairs. Finish chopping the cabbage and the two onions on the table. Fetch more water from the cistern although the barrel in the kitchen is more than half full.

I imagine Monsieur Faure's body as hard and lean, badly scarred on the left side. With skin whiter than his face and neck and forearms, not a lot of hair on his chest. Mademoiselle's body as angles rather than curves. With small, empty breasts, pelvic bones that stick out, a small, saggy derrière.

Julien is skinny, I can feel his bones when he presses against me. I want to draw him without his clothes but don't know how to ask.

I used to listen to my parents making love. Maman would try to shush Papa but he didn't know how to be quiet. He was a noisy man. He spoke loudly, chewed loudly, laughed loudly. Even his movements were loud. I would listen to their lovemaking and imagine them entwined like the lovers I saw in the Bois de Boulogne.

Pierre Faure does not return to Villard de Lans and the villagers' attention shifts from our being spies to Mademoiselle Moreau living in sin. The curé who has ignored us until now pays us a visit but Mademoiselle doesn't invite him in. He is standing at the door when she declares that she stopped believing in God during the last war and isn't about to change her mind in the midst of another one.

Pierre, as he insists I call him, transforms the place. He is as noisy as Papa, and from Mademoiselle's description, as curious as both our fathers. He is always talking, laughing, singing, in spite of the sharp downturn of his mouth.

He soon finds his way around the rest of the house. Comes with me when I line up for food in the village. Small children cry when they see his face. The older children call him names. *Tête fondue*, melted head, is the most popular taunt.

A strange procession starts to make its way to our house above the village. Children, mostly girls, who want piano lessons. Women who want Mademoiselle to write a letter to their sons or husbands who are prisoners of war. Some of them can't write, others can but don't know what to say. A young boy comes with an empty bottle of ink and a rusty pen, hoping we can fill one and replace the other. At first Mademoiselle turns these people away, thinking they are spying on us but they keep coming and she relents. They don't come empty-handed, bringing what they can – a pair of wood-soled *galoches*, a square of Swiss chocolate, a box of matches.

After Monsieur Gauthier hangs his likeness in the boulangerie, several women ask me to sketch them so they can add a drawing to the letters Mademoiselle has helped them draft. No one in the village has a camera. I cut the pages in Monsieur Moreau's sketch pads into quarters so they will fit in the envelopes without being folded. Sometimes the women bring a piece of brown wrapping paper, the end leaf from a book, the inside of a cigarette package. I draw on whatever they give me.

We are lying in the field again. The sky is enormous above us. A medium blue Matisse would love. The clouds have gathered along the ridge and the wind is nudging them down the tree-dense slopes. I remove my hands from under my head, let it sink further in the tall grass so that everything blurs to green.

"Every blade of grass has its angel who bends over it and whispers grow, grow." Julien tells me.

I imagine tiny angels hovering over the grass that surrounds me. Their wings iridescent in the afternoon light. "Who said that?"

"It's in the Talmud."

"What's the Talmud?"

"You should be ashamed of yourself. A Jewish girl who doesn't know about the Talmud."

I sit up, annoyed. "Why should I be ashamed? I know what I know. I am who I am. You only talk to me because you're stuck here. In Paris, you never would've looked at me."

"That's not true."

"And those angels shouldn't be wasting their time on blades of grass when Jews are being hunted down like animals."

I head back to the village but he doesn't try to follow me.

illusion: what we think we have, what we think we've lost
ramille: a small branch, delicate, easily snapped
cloître: cloister, a refuge, the architecture of silence
mal'ach: angel in Hebrew, messenger, intermediary,
God's henchman
papilloner: to flit about like a butterfly, fail to pay
attention, like those grass-blowing angels in the Talmud

My lycée was commandeered by the Luftwaffe. The teachers who hadn't decamped to the countryside organized classes wherever they could. In another lycée, at the mairie, in a church basement. Mademoiselle Moreau taught us composition and literature in her apartment, over the objections of her concierge. She had hung a blackboard and a map of France in her living room. Had arrayed the chairs she had borrowed from her neighbours.

Why a map of France when she didn't teach history or geography? To give a bit of atmosphere, she said when someone asked her the question. She had even smiled.

La Morose smiling and talking about atmosphere. The war really had changed everything.

I sit at the piano, my hands still on my lap. Pierre and Mademoiselle have gone to Villard de Lans with François and will not be back for several hours. I have closed all the windows so that the sound of my playing will not carry.

The lid is already up. Pierre was playing scales while they waited for François and his smell hangs in the air, sweat and cigarette smoke and wood ash from the soap he made yesterday. But it is a whiff of the beeswax Mademoiselle used to polish the piano that almost destroys my resolve. A smell so sweet, so normal, so devastatingly familiar.

I see two pairs of hands on the keyboard. My mother's, elegant and strong, and my five-year-old hands, small and plump. She is wearing her midnight blue dress, a scarf of the same material, and her crystal earrings. I can smell her face powder, her lipstick, her perfume.

I loved that dress, Papa whispers.

As I lift my hands to the keys, I brace myself. My fingers scoff at my apprehension, settling on the well-worn ivories as if they had always known them.

You are breaking my heart, ma chérie, Papa whispers when I stop.

How can I break his heart when he's dead? When I am the one whose heart is broken, whose soul has turned to stone.

"That was extraordinary!" Julien declares from the doorway.

Julien has never come to the house before. He must've seen Mademoiselle and Pierre driving away with François, in the truck that first brought him here.

"Don't be angry. I did knock." He comes to stand behind me and rests his hands on my shoulders. "I thought you said you hadn't touched the piano since you arrived here."

"I haven't."

"So how could you play so flawlessly?"

"I don't know. It flowed through me, like a current."

"And what were you playing?"

"One of my compositions."

"You wrote that? What is it called?"

"Hannah's Lament."

"And who is Hannah?"

"I think she is my mother's sister."

Words are the twigs, bits of grass and bark and leaf we need to
build a nest for what we mean, for what we feel.

I find a picture book of Canada in one of the boxes Mademoiselle
is sorting through. "Jean bought me that book for my twentieth
birthday. We were thinking of emigrating when the war put an
end to our plans."

So it was Jean that she had loved.

I leaf through the pages, try to admire the Saint Lawrence
River, Niagara Falls, the Rocky Mountains, but I can't. We could
be living there now, the three of us, homesick for Paris, for France.
Complaining about the lack of history and culture in our new country. Like Tante Marthe did in every one of her letters.

We could all be in Canada. Together. Safe and sound.

What do you say to that, Papa? You who scoffed at Maman for
worrying. Who thought Jews were safe in France. Who dismissed
Canada as nothing but a backwater.

We talk about Paris, about school, about music, about the war, but
we never discuss our families. Julien hasn't asked me what happened to my parents and I haven't asked him what happened to his.

And yet when we talk the questions swirl around our heads, unasked, unanswered, like moths. When they get too close we shoo them away but they always return, brushing their wings against our cheeks, getting caught in our hair. What is your mother's name? Is your father bald? Do you have sisters or brothers? Who do you miss the most? Do you think they're dead?

> *passerelle*: a narrow bridge, a gangplank,
> the distance between life and death
> *opaque*: without light, obscure, impenetrable
> *artifice*: what is not real, what pretends to be real,
> what ought to be real and isn't
> *seashells*: a whisper of a word that Katou taught me,
> soft as the sand that is their home
> *tefilah*: the word for prayer in Hebrew, as in
> unheard and unheeded

Pierre is laughing. His scars moving grotesquely over his face. I thought I would get used to them but they continue to horrify me.

Mademoiselle nods, as if to encourage me, as if she knows what I want to do.

"May I touch your scars?" I ask Pierre, my eyes still on Mademoiselle's face.

He turns towards me, gropes for my hand. "Yes, but first you must close your eyes. Or you will not be able to appreciate them," he says with a laugh.

He places my hand on his neck. The skin feels waxy and sinewy, like a new leaf. His pulse flutters under my fingertips. I trace the contour of his face, the shape of his ravaged nose, the twist of his mouth. Touch the taut, thick skin over his cheekbones, the softer flaps under his eyes.

His face is like a relief map, a carved mask, a dried-out river bed.

The piano was gone, the matelassé lying in a heap on the floor, my father's sculptures and maquettes destroyed. The paintings that had hung on the walls were gone, the nails they used to hang on still anchored in the plaster. None of the furniture had been taken, too shabby to be of any interest.

My parents' bedroom was torn apart, clothes and books and sheet music strewn on the floor. The mattress lying half off the bed. I took the satin scarf that matched the dress Maman wore to play at the Café Versailles and Papa's paint-stained sarrau.

Hurry, Madame la concierge hissed from the hallway.

The alcove that was my bedroom was also a mess but Papa's drawings of Sainte Marie-Madeleine were still hanging on the wall. I removed them from their frames and rolled them one inside the other. I grabbed my cahiers, my musical compositions, my sketch pad and pencils.

You need clothes, fille. Madame is now standing in the kitchen doorway.

I gathered my other dress and my cardigan from the floor, my night-gown from under the mattress, underwear and socks from a pulled-out drawer.

Where is your winter coat?

Under Maman's bed.

Madame returned with the coat and a suitcase. I lined the bottom with my treasures and placed the clothes over them, with the bulky coat on top. I could feel Madame's impatience, smell her fear.

I take a photograph of my parents, one of me as a baby, and the last letter from Tante Marthe, the one with the picture of my cousin Solange.

We have to go now, before Loïc comes home. He won't hesitate to turn you in. He is just like his father.

I followed her up to the fifth floor, where she had been hiding me for two days, holding on to the handrail, as the steps melted under my feet.

I will bring you some food after my husband and son are asleep. Then in the morning, very early, I will take you to that teacher you mentioned.

"Why did you help me?"

Mademoiselle finishes her row and sets down her knitting. She is making socks with the awful green wool she was unravelling the day I asked her what happened to Pierre in the war.

"Because I could," she answers quietly.

"Did you hide Martine Lévy and her sister? Help them obtain false identity cards?"

She shrugs as if it were nothing.

"Madame la concierge knocked on every door but no one would take me, although my family had lived in the building since I was a baby. She knew her husband would beat her if he found out she had tried to help me, that he was the one who had denounced my parents."

"Your neighbours were afraid her husband would turn on them too."

"You weren't afraid."

"You give me too much credit, child. You came to me, remember? All I had to do was open the door and let you in. Hardly heroic."

"You saved my life."

She shrugs and starts a new row.

cicatrice: a scar, a reminder, benign or
terrifying, fate's signature
baiser: a kiss, a meeting of lips, another
type of signature
constellation: a family of stars, a shape
in the sky, a life pattern
lucarne: a skylight, an unexpected
glimpse of the world
shalom: hello, good-bye, peace, completeness,
health, perfection and more.
Do all Hebrew words carry so much meaning?

"Where will you hide, if they come looking for us?"
"In the pile of metal objects next to the school. The schoolboys
hide in there all the time."
"I'll walk up the stream and then into the woods."
"So you think they will come with dogs?"
"They might."

François brings me a message from Julien and doesn't wait for me
to open it. I hurry upstairs to my room, thinking it is a love note.

My dearest,
I cannot stay here. Not after what happened in Vénissieux. I'm
going to join the partisans. Word is that the Germans will cross into the
Unoccupied Zone before the winter.
Adieu. I will never forget you.
S.

I feel like the piano falling into the valley.

I search for François but I can't find him either. His cabin at the edge of Monsieur Bartoli's farm is empty, his truck gone. Maybe he and Julien have gone off together. When I knock at Madame Grissot's, she parts the curtain but doesn't open the door.

Pierre tells me to stop making enquiries.

"But Julien is too young to fight with the partisans. He's only sixteen."

"He's made his choice. Don't endanger yourself and the others."

"What others?"

"The other children who are hiding in the villages of Quatre Montagnes."

"Are you helping François? Do you know where Julien is?"

Pierre doesn't answer me. I light him a cigarette, place it in his hand, my fingers grazing his ropy scars. He brings the cigarette to his twisted mouth and draws on it.

"What happened in Vénissieux?"

He exhales. The smoke ring floats up, distorted.

"You told me that Julien came here from Lyon. Is this Vénissieux near Lyon?"

He nods. "A few kilometres to the south."

"Is there an internment camp there?"

"A transit camp. They were holding the Jewish children there, the ones they'd rounded up in Paris and Lyon."

"And?"

"About eighty or so were rescued. François was in Lyon visiting his brother who asked him to take ten of them. He brought them here and Monsieur Gauthier found homes for them all."

"What happened to the other children?"

"They were taken away by train."

"Where were they taken?"

"East. That's all we know."

It's getting colder. The mood in the village is sombre now that the Germans have crossed into the Unoccupied Zone. We're isolated here but there are collaborators everywhere. It was a Frenchman who betrayed my parents, a man who used to give me licorice when I was a child.

I retreat into silence. Wander all over the plateau on foot or on Mademoiselle's bicycle. Wearing several of the sweaters Mademoiselle has knitted with the wool we unravelled, my feet warm in all the pairs of stockings I stuff into her boots.

In my dreams, I jump off the cliffs. Dressed all in white, a luminous, shimmering white, I float down, gently, with cahiers trailing behind me, sketches, shells, Maman's scarf. When I try to draw myself floating, I can never get the face right. The joy, the glow on my face, as if an angel is trying to break through the skin. Are Jewish angels different from Catholic ones? What kind of angel is trying to burst out of me?

I wave to Mademoiselle and Pierre (who is waving vigorously in the wrong direction) until l'Hôtel de la Poste disappears from view. Monsieur Gauthier stands in front of the boulangerie in his floured clothes, oblivious to the cold, as the wagon rattles by. Madame Grissot lifts the curtain on her door. There are several people in the wagon, including Monsieur le Maire who has business at the préfecture in Grenoble, as he so loudly informed us once we were all seated. Since François disappeared with his wood-fuelled truck, this is the only way to leave the village.

Monsieur Gauthier has given me his brother's address in Annecy. His brother knows a retired mountain guide who has been taking Jewish children across the border into Switzerland. Maybe I can work with him, help with the little ones. Mademoiselle cried when I told her what I wanted to do but didn't try to stop me. Told me I was old enough to decide how I wanted to live in the world.

The mayor is glaring at me although I take as little room as possible. His eyes narrower and his face pudgier than the day he asked us to dismantle the telescope. I draw the village, the plateau, the clouds gathered on the ridge. The pages of Monsieur Moreau's sketch pad may have yellowed but the Baignol & Farjon pencil is thick and sharp. When I'm done, I write down my first words of the day across the bottom of the drawing:

Quatre Montagnes: rocks and trees and sky, a scattering
of villages, the nature of refuge

ciel: sky, heaven, the beauty of the colour blue

silence: emptiness, the absence of noise,
the sound of God breathing.

GLOSSARY/NOTES – MAL'ACHIM

accordeur	piano tuner
blanchisserie	laundry
cahier	notebook
calepin	pad
cassoulet	bean and meat stew
charcuterie	butcher shop specializing in pork products
citron pressé	lemonade
courgette	zucchini
espionne	spy
grande guerre	the Great War
lavoir public	a communal place to do laundry
Les Halles	large central market in Paris, dismantled in 1971
mairie	town hall
matelassé	quilted cover
papeterie	stationery store
pichet	small carafe
Quatre Montagnes	north end of the massif de Vercors, west of Grenoble
sarrau	smock

BREATHING

No one saves us but ourselves.
No one can and no one may.
We ourselves must walk the path.

THE BUDDHA

I CAN HEAR THEM BREATHING. My brother at the back of the makeshift stage. My son at the lighting console. Chantrea the length of a hand away. I have always been able to hear people breathing, hearts beating. It comes from years of lying quietly as a child, with nothing but the sound of my own breath, my own heart.

The platform smells of sawdust and paint and the cigarettes Daniel smoked as he wielded his saw and brush. The air still bristles with the sound of his hammer, his many expletives. Without him, we would not be here. We would not have a stage, an audience, a second chance.

I deepen my own breathing. Empty my mind. My years with the monks still serve me, still underpin my life.

The *chapei* wails in the small space. It is a startling sound if you are not used to it, like the cry of a wounded tiger. I flinch as the words fall from Chamroeun's mouth, harsh and hard. Words that can twist whatever is straight in you, break whatever is whole.

A light creeps across the floor, up the black painted steps to where I sit. I am leaning forward, an elbow on each knee, my hands hanging loose, my left foot on one step, my right on another. An unlikely Cambodian pose but my son insisted.

I wait for the tiger to slink away before I speak.

Solid. That was my first impression of Canada.
Houses built of brick and stone. Sidewalks. Paved streets.
Even the clothes people were wearing seemed sturdy: parkas and long woolen coats, knitted hats and fur-rimmed hoods, thick boots that looked like they could walk on the moon.

The light shifts to Chantrea and leaves me in darkness. Her voice is strong and delicate, as supple as a bamboo leaf, her French formal, which means she must have studied at a lycée back home. Why have I forgotten this about her?

I must concentrate. Listen to what she is saying instead of how she is saying it. I must not miss my cue.

There were no soldiers, no weapons. No whiff of menace in the air. No dilapidated buildings, no piles of rubble, no garbage on the streets.

I am standing now. Chantrea steps forward, places her hand on my shoulder. I let her words fall into my ears like feathers in a nest.

She auditioned to sing with our band once. We were not expecting her as she had not called or signed the sheet we had posted at the Cambodian Centre. She started to sing while we were putting our instruments away, while we all had our backs to her. A traditional song. Stunned by the strength of her voice, the depth of her sadness, we stayed where we were, sitting on our instrument cases or kneeling on the floor, afraid to move, to turn around, to break the spell. She disappeared as soon as she finished, without leaving her name or number. Chamroeun called her the ghost singer, claimed he was in love with her. I never told him what I knew.

It was still dark when I woke up my first morning in Montreal. I was lying on the floor, beside the bed my sponsors had bought for me, tangled in a comforter that smelled inexplicably of lemons. I must have been jet-lagged, not that I would have known the difference, after so many years of deprivation.

I was not hungry so I made myself a pot of tea. Figured I would buy some noodles from a street vendor later. I pulled on the parka, the boots, the hat and mitts I had been given. Opened the door to a blast of cold air. Went down the icy steps that wound from the third floor to the ground.

It was lighter now. The street was empty and I wondered where all the people were, unfamiliar with the concept of sleeping in, of a day, like Sunday, being different from another.

The wind was cold and sharp. Slashing through my parka like a blade through bamboo. I did not mind the cold – it was just nature being nature. I remembered a different kind of cold, back home, when my brothers and I were digging ditches. We often had to sleep where we were working, too far from camp to return there. At the mercy of the elements and the mosquitoes. Burrowing into the damp slope of the ditch to avoid the water pooled at the bottom. Shivering in the mud while our guards laughed and smoked cigarettes on the embankment.

The chapei wails again but the light stays on me. My brother weaves my words and Chantrea's into his song, sharpening their edges, pressing them into my flesh.

I came to a street lined with shops, none of which were open, and a sidewalk without food carts. I read the various shop signs with the French I pretended not to know under the Khmer Rouge. Stopped in front of the windows, each one displaying something different. Books. Recordings. Clothes. A dizzying array of shoes.

The smell of fresh bread lured me to a side street. The boulanger was standing in his doorway, smoking a cigarette, oblivious to the cold. He waved me in and turned on the lights. Went to stand behind the counter, dropping his cigarette in a battered metal ashtray. I ordered a baguette, placing several bills on the counter, money that my sponsors had given me. The boulanger laughed. Returned all but one of them as well as a coin. The denominations obviously different from what I was used to.

I was reminded of the first baguette I bought when I arrived in Phnom Penh from the countryside, of the old woman who sold it to me. When I stuck the baguette in my mouth instead of tearing a piece off with my hands, she laughed too, her teeth red with betel juice, rattling her basket to prevent flies from landing on her loaves.

I left the bakery and wandered back to the main street. It was so quiet. No vendors barking their wares. No motorcycles, no horns, no *cyclo bells. The few cars that drove by hardly made a noise. All I could hear was the crunch of the snow under my boots, so different from the sucking sound of mud I was used to.*

The light cuts out. Chamroeun plays a lighter air on his flute. I leave the stage as Arun steps onto it, the platform creaking under his considerable weight. Arun is Chantrea's husband. His voice is hard and smooth, like a river stone.

My son is waiting for me, grinning and wet-eyed. Daniel is behind him, almost invisible in his black clothes.

"Merci, merci." Rangsey embraces me, his clipboard digging into my chest. It feels good to hold him, to bridge the distance between us, if only for a moment.

"Your participation means so much to me, Papa. Your narrative is the key to the whole play."

I thought the point was not to have a narrative. Only documentation. Stories told without embellishment, one after another, leaving the people in the audience to construct their own play. This is the theory at least. Daniel laughed out loud when I first told him about it and yet he was the one who saved the project, who offered his café as a venue when the Cambodian Centre cancelled.

"Chamroeun was amazing, man," Daniel tells me once Rangsey has returned to the light board. "I love the way he plays that banjo-thingy, the way he moans out loud. You'd think such caterwauling would break your eardrums instead of your heart..."

Caterwauling. A word I would normally write down in my notebook but I did not bring it with me.

I follow Daniel out the back door and down the alley to a side street. He rolls himself a cigarette and I can see traces of black paint on his fingers when he lights it.

"So how many people are we playing to, Daniel? Fifteen, twenty?" With the light in my eyes, I could not tell.

"Hell no. More like fifty. Every chair I have has a bum on it and there are people standing at the back. All of then clutching DVDs of *The Killing Fields*."

He laughs. He loves to make fun of bleeding hearts although he himself is one and with a bigger heart than most.

"So, tell me about Chantrea."

I hesitate. Which could have gotten me killed under the Khmer Rouge.

"Give it up, man. I've seen the way you look at her. The way she tries not to look at you. So where do you know her from? The refugee camp? Your home village?"

Daniel always asks multiple questions, planting his foot firmly in the door so you cannot close it. I do not answer. I do not trust myself to talk about her.

I owe my life in this country to a small downtown church and its refugee committee. To Monsieur and Madame Tremblay who took such good care of me. Who met me at the airport, settled me in my first apartment, gave me a job in their restaurant.

At first, I cleared tables and washed dishes. Peeled potatoes for french fries, vegetables for the ragoût. But I was soon making everything on the menu, bacon and eggs, hamburgers, sausages, hot sandwiches, ragoût, spaghetti with tomato sauce.

Every morning, when I walked into the diner, they fussed over me. Monsieur would make me sit at the counter while he cooked my breakfast. Bacon and eggs or pancakes. Madame would make me tea, terrible tea I was supposed to drink with milk and sugar. Mange, mange, she would urge me, in her gentle, purring voice.

The Tremblays included me in every part of their lives. They took me shopping. They took me to their doctor, their dentist, their chiropractor. They even took me to church. They knew I was not a Catholic but they figured God was God and He would sort it out. When I tried to explain that the Buddha was not a god, they thought I was just being modest.

When they closed their restaurant for two weeks every summer, they took me to the cottage they always rented on a small lake in the Laurentians. Nobody told them how to treat me. They were practical people, loving people, so they were practical and loving with me.

I went to evening classes twice a week to obtain my high school diploma. The other three evenings, I worked for Monsieur Tremblay's brother who ran the dry-cleaning shop next to the restaurant. Just me, the iron, and a pile of shirts.

Narith and Sopham are next. They are brother and sister and take turns speaking. Their anecdotes about immigrant life are funny rather than poignant but the people in the audience are afraid to laugh. I step off the stage. Arun and Chantrea are drinking coffee in the narrow hallway, standing back to back. This is how I like to think of them, together but apart, although I have no right to think of them at all.

I have a wife and son.
A good job, teaching French as a second language.
Enough. More than enough to eat.
I live in a solid house, on a solid street, in a solid city, in a solid country which is not about to abolish money and private property. Ban religion. Execute musicians and artists. A country which is not about to close its schools and hospitals, empty its cities, and murder its citizens.

I teach French to immigrants. My students come from different backgrounds and vary greatly in age and occupation. I can have *a cardiologist from Mongolia sitting beside a sheepherder from Peru. A teenager from Senegal beside a grandmother from Lebanon. I was enrolled in such a class myself when I first arrived in Montreal but they soon transferred me to the CEGEP because my French was too advanced.*

I recognize myself in my students. I know how to help them, how to encourage them. Yes, even how to console them.

I step to the edge of the platform as everyone gathers behind me.

When we were young, my brothers and I would press ourselves on the muddy bank of the river and leave impressions of our bodies. The way children here make angels in the snow. We would then trade places and stretch or shrink to fit the imprint of someone else's body.

Little did we realize that one day we would be living in someone else's country.

Living in someone else's country is a lot like living in someone else's body. The parts are the same: arms, legs, hands, feet, mouth. You walk, you sit, you eat, you talk but it does not feel like your body.

It does not feel like your life.

I leave the stage and the café after my last monologue. Catch a bus home before Rangsey and Daniel realize I'm gone. Not that the ordeal is over. There are two more evenings to be endured.

The bus is crowded, noisy; the lights too bright. I keep my eyes closed. Concentrate on my breathing. I can do this. I can do this without breaking down.

The house is mercifully empty. My wife has gone to stay with her sister, to protest what our son is doing. "The Cambodian Centre was right to cancel your play," she screamed at him. "You are exploiting our suffering, our shame."

Sothea will not stay away for long but I appreciate her absence. The way the house feels without her in it.

Rangsey and I walk up to Mont Royal as we do most Saturday afternoons. I am surprised that he came today, thought he would be too busy with the play.

It was Monsieur Tremblay's brother who first brought me here, soon after I started ironing shirts at his dry-cleaning shop. I remember sitting in the back of his blue Parisienne, wedged between the two Madame Tremblays, the smell of their cigarettes and their hairspray in my nose, their gossip like monkey chatter in my ears. The two brothers in the front seat talking about René Levesque and the results of the sovereignty referendum, which was even more incomprehensible.

From the moment I stepped out into the park, I felt better. The sun seemed warmer on my face, the grass greener under my feet. The air to flow more freely through my lungs.

"Why did you leave half way through?" Rangsey is asking. "You missed the best part. The applause. The people who gathered around to congratulate us. It was awesome."

"I am happy for you."

"Maybe you can stay longer this evening."

"This evening will be difficult. Much more difficult. Even if I am not on stage."

He stops to scribble something in his notebook. I know he heard me.

"Maman called just as I was leaving the apartment."

My heart narrows. If Sothea has broken her silence, it means she will be home soon. She is predictable, even in her absences.

"She didn't ask about the play but she wanted to know about Chantrea."

It is not enough that I am in his play, that he has me talking about the past in front of strangers, now he wants to pry into my private life. As we reach the first fork in the path, I veer left instead of right. Walking around the park has lost its allure.

"Where are you going? We just got here!"

Rangsey soon overtakes me, grabs my arm. "Wait. Why is Maman asking about Chantrea?"

What can I tell him? That I still long for the woman I wanted to marry instead of his mother? That he has sharpened that longing by pairing me with her in his play?

"Papa?"

Rangsey will not let this go. Even as a boy, he never just asked, he insisted on knowing. Why the sky was blue, why the garbage can smelled, why we gave names to dogs and cats and not to bees and spiders.

"Chantrea answered the same notice your mother did. The one I posted at the Cambodia Centre, looking for a wife."

"And?"

"I married your mother."

"But you loved Chantrea? Is that why Maman won't come and see the play?"

The play. That's all he cares about.

"Why is she ranting about it then?"

"I do not think ranting is a respectful word to use when speaking of your mother."

Rangsey mumbles something about his mother getting the respect she deserves. This is what they think here, that parents have to earn the respect of their children. I have never gotten used to it.

It starts to rain, a cold sharp rain which still has a touch of winter in it. Rangsey pulls up his hood and I unfurl my umbrella. We head down into the city, the sound of our footsteps our only conversation.

The play project runs over three evenings. Yesterday we talked about immigrant life in Montreal; tonight, it will be the Khmer Rouge. Tomorrow, life in Cambodia before the troubles.

Word of mouth has been positive. There are many more people lined up than can fit in the café. One of them is a reporter from Radio-Canada, which will please Rangsey. I am standing outside myself, as I have only come to support my son this evening, not to participate.

Saint Laurent is noisy, bustling like any Friday night. I wander down the block, peer into restaurants and storefronts, sidestep couples walking arm in arm, talking and laughing. There is a giddiness in the air, after the long cold winter, even if there are no signs of its imminent demise. When I head back to Daniel's café, I see Rangsey pacing out front, his clipboard in hand.

"Oh there you are, Papa. I've been looking for you. I need you to talk about the evacuation of Phnom Penh. Phirun refuses to do it."

The evacuation of Phnom Penh. How casually he asks me this, like he is ordering from a take-out menu. One evacuation, two work camps, a side order of torture.

"I do not want to talk about the Khmer Rouge, Rangsey. You will have to find someone else."

"There is no one else. And I can't leave out the evacuation. The rest of the storyline depends on it."

The rest of the storyline. He is thinking only of his play, not the people who animate it, who live with this storyline, whether there is an audience or not.

He hurries away, knowing I will comply.

I went to Phnom Penh to attend the lycée there. I lived with my sister and her husband in a rattan shack with a dirt floor, so different from the houses in our village. My brother-in-law, who had lost his job when the government fell, drank a lot and mistreated my sister, ashamed of his reduced circumstances.

The lycée was in poor shape. The stucco walls were crumbling, the paint was peeling off the shutters, the roof was leaking. Even the teaching was chaotic. We never knew which teacher we would have or for how long. Some disappeared for weeks at a time. They tried to interest me in the Khmer Rouge but after years of living with monks, I was not interested in more dogma.

When the Khmer Rouge seized the capital, they ordered the evacuation of Phnom Penh. My sister refused to leave without her husband who had obeyed an earlier summons for government employees to report to work. A summons I had urged him to ignore. Knowing enough about the Khmer Rouge to be worried.

The evacuation order made no sense. I did not believe the propaganda on the radio, that the Americans were about to bomb Phnom Penh, even though they had bombed my village eighteen months earlier. Why were the Khmer Rouge closing down a city of almost two million people? It could only be sinister.

My sister packed food for my journey: rice wrapped in banana leaves, dried fish, and preserves from her mother-in-law's garden. I filled some plastic jugs with water from the pump at the end of our alley and watched with dread as masses of people trudged down the street. By the time I returned to the house, Nakry was waiting for me, her few belongings in a bag, ready to follow her brother-in-law home. When I begged her to come with me instead, she refused. Told me she would be safe with her husband's family. We embraced and I took my leave, my heart heavier than the load I carried.

Even though I was travelling alone, I did not make good progress on the first day. There was too much chaos on the streets, too many people who needed assistance, carts that had to be righted, loads that had to be rebalanced. I kept my eyes and ears open, as my French teacher had once advised me to do. What I saw and heard was as implausible as the evacuation itself.

I carried a small boy on my back for a while and shared my food with him and his mother. Accompanied them to their village although it was out of my way. Her family offered me food and a mat for the night. The next day they sent me off with provisions for the rest of my journey.

Chantrea is next but I do not stay. I do not want to hear her talk about her first husband, a journalist, who died in the chaos of the evacuation.

Daniel is waiting for me and he's scowling.

"What the fuck were you doing on stage?"

"I had to replace Phirun at the last minute. He refused to talk about the evacuation. "

"Smart man."

My eyes stray from David's face. I am worried that Phirun has gone home. That I will have to replace him all evening.

"What if you had a flashback on stage? And people thought it was part of the play? How traumatic would that be?"

"So you are a psychiatrist now?"

"You don't have to be a shrink to figure out the downside to this reality show."

"The play is not a reality show."

"Of course it is. It's just morbid instead of stupid. On stage instead of on the boob tube."

"It is a documentary theatre project."

"Fancy name, same game. It's one thing to talk about your experience as an immigrant or your childhood in Cambodia. But to describe what happened to you under the Khmer Rouge, in public like this, is fucking reckless."

Rangsey appears, pale and agitated. "Phirun is gone. He's taken Srey and Moeuk with him. Nhean, Kosal and Prak never showed up."

"Maybe we should close it down," Daniel says.

"Who is still here?" I ask.

"Narith, Sopham. Arun and Chantrea."

"We can manage between us. Tonight was bound to be the most difficult. We cannot close it down, Daniel. It will make the play ineligible for that competition. Which is why you offered us a venue in the first place. Why you built us this stage."

Daniel reluctantly agrees.

When I finally reached my home village, my parents were surprised to see me. They knew nothing of what was going on in Phnom Penh and were puzzled by all the city people streaming through the market town. I tried to tell them what I had learned on the road. That the Khmer Rouge had evacuated all the cities, not just Phnom Penh. That they had abolished money. Banned religion. Forbidden music. My father and uncles did not believe any of it. Dismissed it all as rumour. Panic. When I suggested they hide their musical instruments, they laughed.

Several families from the city settled in our village and built crude huts down by the river. They kept to themselves until the communal kitchens were set up and we were forced to eat together.

When officials came looking for musicians to play at a patriotic rally in the market town, my father and uncles volunteered although I had warned them not to respond to such requests. They loaded their instruments in the back of the truck and waved at us as it pulled away. We never saw them again.

A few months later these same officials identified me as an intellectual for having attended the lycée in the city (I was betrayed by someone in my village) and sent me to a work camp farther up the river. I was not killed because I was the son of peasants and considered untainted.

When I was assigned to dig irrigation ditches, I met up with two of my brothers. The work was arduous, the rice insufficient. We had to attend meetings every evening at which they tried to indoctrinate us, to trick us into betraying ourselves. You could be punished for just about anything. For wearing glasses. Humming while working. For knowing how to speak French. How to play an instrument.

When they asked for someone to play the flute to accompany the patriotic songs at the end of each meeting, my brothers and I stared straight ahead, like all the others. Nobody could accuse us of not learning the new rules.

I move my hand across my knees. The signal for the light to cut out. I speak into the darkness.

Mud.

Near the river it smelled of fish and decaying vegetation; on the road it smelled of bamboo and cow dung.

In the work camps, when we were digging irrigation ditches, the mud stank of sulphur and death.

The light returns. The words flow out of me. I do not censor them, relying on Rangsey to cut the light if I start to ramble.

When I went back to our village on a two-day pass, I found strangers living in our house, my mother in one of the crude huts by the river. Too weak to work in the fields, she would have perished if the city people had not taken her in. They had been protecting her for two months, sharing their meagre rations with her.

Meh asked for news of my father and brothers and cried when I told her that I had been digging ditches with Ponleak and Savuth. She told me that my sisters were still in the market town but their husbands had been taken away. When I asked her if she had news from Nakry in Phnom Penh, she lowered her eyes. I knew I should never have left her behind.

I gave her some broth. She talked about my childhood, my fragile health. A smile on her chapped lips, a spark in her wounded eyes. She told me how she carried me in a sling on her back until I was four years old. How I used to fall asleep with my face in her hair, a strand in each hand. How relieved she was when I recovered my health and found my way in the world.

She held each detail to the light, as if she wanted to see it clearly one last time before she placed it in her krama for safekeeping. Her voice was so weak I had to lean forward to catch her words. My sister Channary arrived the day I had to leave, the first time she had been allowed back in three months and I was grateful to see her again, to leave Meh in her care. I stubbornly believe that my mother died in Channary's arms, that she was not alone when her time came.

I withdraw as Narith and Sopham settle on the stage. Chamroeun strums the chapei, his voice rising in complaint, a voice so like my father's it brings pain to my heart. The chapei was our father's instrument and we cannot listen to it without thinking of him, without wondering what happened to him.

Rangsey is waiting for me as I am now responsible for the final scene of tonight's performance and he needs to adjust the lighting sequences and the musical interludes.

We woke up, stiff and hungry, as we did every morning. But it was not like the other mornings. It was quiet. No slogans on the loudspeaker. No gunfire in the distance.

There was no breakfast either. The pots were empty, the fires unlit.

We looked at each other, which was also unusual. We never looked at anybody. We never knew when someone was going to betray us.

"They're gone," someone said, "and they took all the food."

We were not surprised. We no longer had the capacity to be surprised.

Some men headed for the road while others chose to walk along the river. I wondered where my brothers were, if they were even together, and what direction I should take to meet up with them again.

"Come with me," one of the men suggested. I followed him to the road, where he turned left, without hesitation, as if he knew where he was going.

"My name is Vannak," he said. I did not offer mine in return.

The stranger was kind to me. Helped me up when I stumbled. Slowed down when I could not keep pace. He eventually pulled a flute out of his pocket and handed it to me. "Found this in the storage shed. Your brothers told me how beautifully you play."

I did not take it. Afraid it was some kind of trap.

"Do you know where my brothers were taken?"

"No. There were work camps all along the river. They could have gone to any one of them. Together or not."

He stood on the side of the road and played the flute. The people who gathered to listen to him did so with tears in their eyes. Music had been banned for so long. They gave us what they could, leaving it on the krama Vannak had spread on the ground. A little bit of rice, a half-eaten fruit, some mushrooms. I scoured the sides of the road for things we could barter with. Found an old bucket, a bicycle pedal, a radio antenna. We used the bucket to catch fish in the river.

"Where are we going?" I finally asked.

"To Thailand," Vannak said.

We walked for days. Met some Vietnamese soldiers who shared their rations with us. One of them gave us the canteen he had taken from a dead soldier.

It took us many more days to reach the border. When we were turned away at the first checkpoint, we had to gamble on a more dangerous path, strewn with mines and dead bodies. Vannak insisted on walking ahead of me.

"Step where I step and nothing will happen to you."

"Why are you doing this? Why are you helping me?"

"I did terrible things. I deserve to die. If I get you into Thailand, my karma will improve."

We finally crossed the border. Vannak left me outside the first camp, told me not to look back. "It will be safer for you that way." He handed me the flute. "May you live all the days of your life."

I lift a different flute to my lips. I can see Chantrea standing by the stage with Arun. There are tears in her eyes.

By the third evening, the makeshift stage feels familiar, the way I sit completely natural. Chamroeun is on the bamboo xylophone tonight and the members of our band have joined us, playing various traditional instruments.

My name is Samnang which means lucky, a name I was given when I was four years old. My father changed my name in the hope that it would change my fate, that it would restore me to health, as I was sickly and small for my age. He also gave me his first name as my last name, to show how much he cared for me. Not that it altered what people actually called me, which was Poeu, little one, a common nickname for the last child in a family.

The new names did not have the desired effect. I remained weak and sickly. Since I was growing too heavy for my mother to carry, my father rigged a small wagon which could be pulled into the rice paddy when everyone was working there. My brothers often carried me on their backs when they went into the forest to gather firewood or down to the river to fish.

Meh gave me small tasks like operating the rice pestle or slicing reeds into strips for her weaving. I also tended the vegetable garden, dipping my bowl in the water we stored in large clay jars under the house and pouring it on the plants, stopping to rest at the end of each row. In the dry season the garden had to be watered three times a day.

When I was too tired, I would rest in the shade of the sugar palm. I wanted so much to climb this tree as my father and brothers did, not to collect the sap from its flowers, but to catch a glimpse of the wider world.

When I was eight, I made a miraculous recovery, all the more miraculous since no one could claim responsibility for it. No extra prayers had been said, I had not been taken to see a doctor in the city, and the khru khmer, our village healer, had been dead for two years.

My recovery, though miraculous, was gradual. I slept less. I seemed to breathe more easily. My appetite improved. I found I could water two rows of plants without taking a rest, walk to the edge of the rice paddy, carry small loads. I did not mention my newfound energy nor did my parents, in case the spirits changed their minds.

My family doctor here thinks I might have had a heart valve problem which corrected itself. Whatever it was, its disappearance transformed my life. I started to eat like there was a ravenous spirit in my stomach. Luckily there was a good rice harvest that year and the river was teeming with fish.

I was not only hungry for food but for movement. I ran clumsily at first but was soon running everywhere. Down to the river and back again, along the elevated pathways between the rice paddies, to the temple at the other end of the village. I helped my father and brothers, eager to take on new chores. Learned to fetch the water from the river, to feed and care for our cow and pig, to fish with my brothers. And I climbed the sugar palm, scrambling up the bamboo rungs my father had fastened to it. I loved to look at the world from up there. The green fields, the river, the mountains in the distance. The world was indeed larger than I had ever imagined.

Poh invited all our relatives and everyone in the village to celebrate my recovery. The women gathered outside our house to make the food while the men built a temporary stage for the music-making. The musicians, including my father and uncles, started to play before the stage was even finished.

I ran around the tables with the other children while my sisters and cousins decorated them with garlands made with banana leaves and hibiscus. When Meh sent my brothers fishing, I stayed behind, afraid I would miss something. In the past, I had to stay in the house during such celebrations, too weak to enjoy all the noise and activity.

After my brothers returned with their baskets full, Meh wrapped the fish in banana leaves and grilled them over the fire. My sisters set out platters of pork, bowls of rice, pots of sour fish soup. Arranged slices of pineapple, papaya and watermelon, and mounds of num treap, sweet sticky rice sprinkled with coconut and sesame.

That night I leaned against the stage and listened to my father play his bamboo xylophone while my sisters, my cousins, and other girls from the village danced. I remember the incense, the delicate hand gestures, the shadows cast by the dancers as the torches flickered all around us. Later in the evening, my father picked up his chapei and started to chant in his rasping voice.

The next day Poh gave me the flute his father had carved out of bamboo and decorated, which he had played as a boy. He had saved *it for me all these years. For the day I would be well and have enough breath to play it.*

I bring the flute Rangsey brought me back from Cambodia to my lips. Chamroeun is back at the bamboo xylophone. We play a song our father may have played on that long ago evening.

I cannot remember my mother's face. My brother tells me to look in the mirror, that I resemble my mother so much I could have been her twin in another life. She is there, in the shape of your eyes, my brother insists, in the contours of your face, in the curl of your hair. I envy him that knowledge, the picture of her he carries in his mind.

Our memories are not reliable. We were so hungry that we imagined all kinds of things as we cleared rattan in the forest or dug another ditch. Meals we never ate, girls we never touched, places we had never been to.

I remember an evening when we were still many under the family roof. My brothers and sisters were sleeping, my father was smoking his pipe outside. My mother was praying in a fervent whisper in front our little altar, holding several incense sticks between her palms. Her face glowing in the candlelight, her hair loose like a girl's. She was sitting with her legs folded to one side and I could see the soles of her feet in the moonlight. The feet are supposed to be impure yet I found them beautiful that night, small and delicate, like tiny folded wings.

The light dims and I step off the platform. The xylophone is strangely silent. I find Chamroeun backstage, huddled in a corner, staring into space. I crouch beside him, try to comfort him. I should not have shared such an intimate memory of our mother. I have caused him pain.

We are surrounded by people waiting to get on stage. I hear Arun asking Chantrea a question, her soft reply. As I shift my weight, I steady myself by putting my hand on the floor. Chantrea brushes against it with her foot. I leave my hand there and she touches it again, trailing the front of her leather slipper across the spread of my fingers.

There was no school in our village, the closest one was four kilometres away, in the market town. My father sent my brothers to live with the monks for a time so they would receive a little education. Chamroeun stayed two years. Of my sisters, only Channary went to school, and only because a cousin of my mother's had moved to the town.

After the rice harvest that year, Poh sent me to live with the monks, in spite of my protestations and those of my mother. I was only ten, four years younger than my brothers were when they were sent. I wanted to live in a larger world, not a smaller one.

I found life in the temple difficult because Meh had always indulged me, even after I recovered my health. The monks were strict, the work arduous. But what I hated the most was begging for food, praying for hours on end.

I lived only for the hours of study. I never tired of copying sentences on my slate, learning multiplication tables, listening to tales from the Gatiloke. We were taught to chant in Pali and Sanskrit and beaten when we mangled or forgot the unfamiliar words. I was the only boy who loved the strange sounds, the way they vibrated in my throat and heart, but I was beaten just as mercilessly as the others.

When I worked in the vegetable garden, I would fix my eyes on the sugar palms in the distance, especially the one that swayed above the roof of my parents' house. I missed my family, especially my mother, and the freedom to move about once my chores were done.

I had been at the wat for two years when a monk arrived from the city. He had lived in France for thirty years until a voice instructed him to return home and become a monk. After he was ordained in Phnom

Penh, the city of his birth, the voice urged him to find a temple in the country so he walked out of the city and was guided to our humble village.

He offered to teach me French. Told me my musical ear would be an advantage, that learning a language was like learning music, just a different set of sounds. I took to French like I took to running after all my years of lying still. Could not get enough of it. I recited poems instead of prayers in my head, wrote out conjugations on my slate, sought new words in my teacher's dictionary. As I learned to read French, I was fascinated by the spaces between the words, spaces we did not have in Khmer except at the end of a sentence.

I decided I would study at a lycée and travel to France as my teacher had done, although I had never been farther than the market town and had no sense of my own country, let alone a different country on another continent. I had never even seen a barang, a white person.

As I leave the stage, Arun strides onto it. Rangsey must have changed the order of the scenes. I find Chantrea beside the platform, listening to her husband's account, as if she had never heard it before.

"Why did you choose him instead of me?" I ask, across the years that lie between us.

She does not turn around. "You know I did not choose Arun. That my aunt arranged the marriage."

"But you could have escaped him by marrying me! Which is why you answered my notice in the first place."

"I did not realize you had placed it."

"You would have preferred another stranger?"

"I was too old for you, Samnang. Too damaged. I could not have more children. It would not have been fair."

As if living without her all these years has been any fairer.

We hear Arun's heavy footfall on the stage. Chantrea disappears so quickly I think I have imagined our conversation.

The world, as I surveyed it when I climbed my first sugar palm, was destroyed in 1973. I was cutting rattan in the forest with another boy when we heard the American B-52. I ran deeper into the forest while the other boy headed back to the wat. That impulse saved my life. Half the village was obliterated, including the wat. My French teacher, any monk who was not out begging for food, and the boys I had studied with were all killed.

In the folds of my robe was a letter the teacher had given me that morning, confirming my acceptance at a lycée in Phnom Penh, a letter I should not have had on my person.

Although more B-52s flew overhead, the rest of our village and the rice paddy we cultivated with seven other families were spared. At the end of September, my father arranged for a cousin to take me to my sister's house in the city. As we reached the ruins of the wat, I stopped for a moment to reflect, to honour the monk who had changed my life.

As I leave the stage for the last time, I encounter Arun and Chantrea on the stairs. She will not look at me. He shakes my hand. I am relieved that it's over, that I do not have to revisit the past for my son or for anyone else. I have always moved forward, crossed chasms without looking down. Rangsey has never understood this.

I leave the café. Get lost in the crowd on the boulevard.

People talk and laugh and jostle me.

I feel lost. Alone. Abandoned.

I sit on the sofa in the Tremblays' living room beside their deaf and arthritic dog. The sofa is covered in dog hair and reeks of the poor animal's many accidents. The Tremblays are ensconced in their recliners, in front of the television I bought for them last month. Madame Tremblay has hidden Cheezies in her knitting basket and slips one in her mouth whenever Monsieur Tremblay is not looking.

Hiding food from her husband is an old habit. At the restaurant she would take chocolate bars from the display case and slip them in her apron pocket, keep bags of chips and Cheezies in the cleaning cupboard. If her husband scolded her for eating too much, she laughed and patted his cheek, pushing whatever she was having under the counter, out of sight.

Monsieur Tremblay has heard about the play on Radio-Canada. He is dabbing his eyes with a handkerchief. "You must be so proud of your boy."

"Why didn't you tell us about the play?" Madame Tremblay asks, wiping her orange fingers on her apron before handling the wool.

"It is an experimental play. People sitting or standing on stage, telling their stories, one interspersing another."

"Doesn't sound very experimental."

"It is improvised. There are no professional actors. No script. No dialogue."

"We'd still like to see it. Maybe you could stage it at the church. Everyone on the refugee committee would come."

Madame Tremblay leans forward to touch my arm, causing the knitting basket to tip over and spill its contents on the floor.

"Huguette. Not more junk food!" Monsieur Tremblay chides in the same worried tone he used at the restaurant. As I crawl on the floor to retrieve the wool, trying not to crush any Cheezies under my knees, I find the carpet as filthy as the sofa. I must come back with Rangsey, give the place a thorough cleaning.

"And how is your lovely wife?" Madame Tremblay asks as if the forbidden Cheezies had not tumbled onto the carpet. "Is she as proud of Rangsey as you are?"

"Yes, very proud." I settle back on the dirty couch.

"Why don't we watch the movie, Samnang," Madame Tremblay suggests. "I hope it's as funny as the last one you brought."

I always bring a comedy. I love to sit on the floor between them, their laughter splashing on me like water from a fountain.

It is late. The moon has risen, round and full, a good omen for the play's opening night at the Cambodian Centre. Not that I believe in omens, good or bad, anymore. I am sitting on my front porch, in case Daniel stops by.

I hear his muffler before the car reaches our block.

"Where were you?" Daniel asks as I come down the steps to greet him. "I was worried. It's not like you to fink out on your son."

"I was following your advice."

"And what advice is that? It flows out of me like piss so you can't expect me to keep track of it."

I pour him tea from a thermos. I do not invite him inside. Sothea is watching TV in our small living room and we would not be able to talk.

"I was first putting myself."

Daniel laughs at the inversion, as I knew he would. "And how did that feel?"

"Not as liberating as I thought it would be. I am miserable actually. And ashamed. I have disappointed my son."

"He'll get over it."

"You do not understand."

"Yes, I do. I have four children, two ex-wives, and a father who is still mad at me for not following in his footsteps. I could give seminars on disappointing people."

He sits on the top step beside me and pulls out his tobacco pouch and a packet of rolling papers. "It was standing room only at the Cambodian Centre. And the people who cancelled the play three months ago were sitting in the front row, looking solemn and important, like the whole thing was their idea."

I know better than to ask if Chantrea was there.

Daniel sprinkles more tobacco on his jeans than on the paper. "I thought I would understand a word here and there but my Khmer is even more pathetic than I thought. I did feel everything that was being said, though, and that was freaky enough."

He rolls the cigarette back and forth between his thick fingers and I turn away before he seals the edge. I always find that part too intimate. As if I am glimpsing the boy in him, the one who stuck his tongue out when his father was not looking.

"Rangsey changed the order, presented the Khmer Rouge stuff first, which I wasn't expecting. Projecting black and white photos across the back of the stage. But when people started making a loud, clicking sound at the back of their throats, a kind of *tsst-tsst*, I thought they were booing, that the play was a flop. It was Chantrea who assured me, at the intermission, that they were just commiserating with the storytellers, feeling their pain."

I keep my face impassive, my eyes on the porch across the street.

"Some people came up to me, afterwards, to shake my hand and thank me again for what I had supposedly done for the Cambodian community."

"Supposedly?"

"Haven't you ever wondered why I chose to study Cambodian refugees?"

"No."

"That's what I like about you, Sam. You don't try to second-guess people."

"Second-guess?"

"You don't judge people, don't presume you know them."

"Is that what you think?"

"That's why I became a sociologist so I could second-guess people in a big way..."

He pauses. I can hear him breathing, his heart beating, the blood pounding in his ears.

"But I ended up exploiting them. Exploiting refugees to advance my career. I knew I would get the funding, Sam. That there were big bucks to be had. From the feds, from the province, from all us bleebs out there."

"Bleebs?"

"A combination of bleeding hearts and plebes."

"You wrote an important book on the integration of refugees."

"I wrote a book. Only time will tell if it was important."

"What about your Order of Canada?"

"I didn't fucking deserve it."

"You cannot reject all your work, Daniel, just because your motivation was not pure. Perhaps you retired too soon."

"Retired? I'm busier now than when I was teaching."

"You are busy, yes, but you also have too much time to think, to second-guess yourself."

He laughs. "That was a quick uptake."

"Uptake?"

"You've already incorporated second-guess in your vocabulary."

"Old habit."

"Not a bad one, I guess. But after twenty five years in the country, you could just relax, you know. Stop writing words in your little notebook. Most words can be understood from the context."

"Not if the context has changed."

"Is that how it still feels?"

"Perhaps you are only allowed one context per lifetime."

Daniel finally lights the cigarette. Passes it to me. Rolls himself another one.

I used to smoke with him in his office, every morning, before he interviewed his first refugee of the day. Afraid of the work that lay ahead of me. Interpreting other people's memories, moving back and forth between Khmer and French and sometimes English, standing too close to the chasm not to look down.

I slide the eggs onto my son's plate, the way Monsieur Tremblay taught me, and they spin ever so slightly before they settle between the baked beans and the home fries. I sit across from him with my tea.

"Why didn't you come last night?"

"I have already explained why."

"But it was the opening night of my play!"

"I was at the opening night of your play. I was *in* your play."

"I know, Papa, but that was more like a dress rehearsal. In front of a bunch of bleeding hearts–"

"I do not like that expression, Rangsey. It is disrespectful. The people who came to see the play are the kind of people who sponsored Cambodian refugees by the hundreds. Including your mother and me, my brother and your mother's sister. And no one who participated in your theatre project would appreciate you calling it a dress rehearsal."

"I spent two years of my life creating a testimonial to what happened over there. Is that not respect enough?"

"You did not live through it so you do not realize what you have been asking of us."

"I was asking you to bear witness. Is that so terrible?"

I stare at the eggs on his plate. They are getting cold.

"Look at me when I'm talking to you."

My son is young. Angry. He wants to change the world. I never tried to change the world. I did not know you could.

Posters for my son's theatre project line the corridors of the Cambodian Centre which is located in the basement of the church that first sponsored us. We have not graduated to our own building although sporadic attempts have been made to raise money for one.

I have not been here with my band since the play opened and several people seek me out at the intermission to congratulate me on my son's project. Which delays me from reaching the back of the room where Chantrea has set up her table. Her uncle has a catering business and she often helps him out.

She pours me a glass of mango juice. "The play is generating a lot of interest, Samnang."

I can only nod. What I planned to say has evaporated.

"I work in the office twice a week and we have received many phone calls from other communities who want to stage a version of it. The War Museum in Ottawa called on Thursday."

"I know. It is very gratifying."

"And what do you think of the new production?"

She talks to me formally, as though she barely knows me.

I sit down on a folding chair, cross my legs to hide how much they are shaking. "I have not seen it."

"You should. It sounds different in Khmer, more natural, especially the scenes set in Cambodia. There are a lot more players, almost thirty, so it is less personal, less intimate, but no less powerful."

Intimate.

"Why did you sing for us?" The question surprises me as I had not intended to ask it.

She crushes the plastic glass in her hand.

"Please. Tell me."

She retreats behind the table to serve one of my bandmates who throws me a look. They are waiting for me to resume the set. All those people who stopped to congratulate me have eroded the few minutes I had with her.

"I was coming out of a meeting," she starts, as I get up to leave. "I could hear the music down the hall and stopped on my way by. You were auditioning the last singer. A young man with a good voice, a badly fitting suit, and shiny black shoes. After he left, I walked across the room but you were busy putting your instruments away, talking and laughing, and never heard me. When I got to the bottom of the steps, where you could not see me, I started to sing. I did not plan it, any of it."

"I knew it was you even though I had never heard you sing."

The lights dim and I return to the stage. I can see the white tablecloth at the back of the room but not Chantrea. She must be sitting on that folding chair. Later, as we are ending our set, I choose the ballad Chantrea surprised us with that day.

As soon as we strum the music, everyone gathers near the stage to sing along. Chantrea's voice is so strong, so haunting, people stop singing to listen to her. My brother glares at me.

"You knew it was her, didn't you?"

When I look for her afterwards, she has vanished. The table is bare, her boxes gone. I drop Chamroeun at his apartment and drive up to Mont Royal in his van, the instruments rattling in the back. I find the noise comforting, imagine a jumble of notes at the bottom of each case, shaken loose by the roughness of the road.

I park in my favourite spot, where I can see the lights of the city, although I have little interest in them tonight. I sit on the hood of the van, in my suit, feeling as exposed as I did on the stage that Daniel built, although there is no one up here but me.

Why did I put Chantrea at risk like that? What will Arun think, for he is bound to hear about it? And Sothea? She will scream at me. Hurl accusations I only wish were true.

What was I thinking, playing that song, tempting fate like that?

Fate.

I found Chantrea wandering in a daze, carrying her boy, during the evacuation of Phnom Penh. Without food or water. Her clothes were splattered with her husband's blood. He had been shot for taking photographs of the evacuation. Passers-by had taken his camera, the food and water he was carrying, while she and the boy were weeping beside his body. They must have been on the edge of the crowd or they would have been trampled.

I shared my rice and fish with them, my jug of water. Offered to carry the boy on my back. Chantrea was stumbling behind me, sobbing, so I had to take her arm, to keep her near me, so she would not get lost in the crowd. It took us more than two days to reach her village.

Kiri was three, maybe four years old. A lovely boy. I do not know how he died or when, Chantrea has never told me.

Sometimes I can hear Kiri breathing. His heart beating.

Feel his little arms around my neck.

His feet as they press against the palms of my hands.

GLOSSARY/NOTES – BREATHING

barang	white person
krama	traditional scarf
Gatiloke	a compendium of Cambodian tales
wat	temple

ON THE BANK OF THE AKANYARU RIVER

Turi bene mugabo umwe.

We are the sons and daughters
of the same father.

RWANDAN SAYING

I CLIMBED INTO THE AGASEKE *and pulled the lid over me. It was cozy inside. The basket rough against my skin. Dark, but not scary dark, since bits of light were seeping through the coiled rows. It smelled like a new basket always smelled, woodsy and damp, the papyrus reeds still holding their wet memories of home.*

Nyogokuru was calling for me outside.

Do-mi-tille. Do-mi-tille.

Scattering the syllables of my name to the wind as she circled the house. When she reached the shed where I was hiding, where she stored her baskets before she took them to market, she checked the smallest baskets first, the ones I could not possibly fit into.

"Domitille," she whispered loudly as she lifted each lid, "you are scaring your grandmother. What will your Papa say if I do not find you before he gets home?"

When she lifted the lid on the basket where I was hiding, I jumped up and wrapped my arms around her. As I pressed my ear to her big bosom, I could hear the first vibrations. Muted at first, then louder and deeper, as from the tautest of drums.

Laughter fit for an umugabekazi.

A queen.

Papa was so excited about the teaching position he had been offered in Canada he could not stop grinning, his big teeth spilling out of his mouth, his eyes ablaze as he shouted *Je ne peux pas le croire* over and over. We could not believe it either. That Papa had found work in our new country. That our emigration was now assured.

My father slapped Clément on the back as if he had just won a match, planted a kiss on my forehead, and danced around the table with Félicité on his shoulders. Maman was smiling and crying as she fed the baby the *isombe* she had made to celebrate the good news. It was our grandmother who usually prepared this dish, who haggled over the price of cassava leaves and aubergines at the market, but Nyogokuru had spent the afternoon crying, too upset by Papa's news to prepare anything.

When Papa finally sat down to eat, he praised the *isombe* so many times Nyogokuru hissed at him. We were so used to Papa swallowing his food without tasting it, his face sombre, his eyes thick with worry, we sometimes forgot how exuberant he could be. How optimistic. How determined to change our fate.

As soon as he finished eating, he pushed his bowl aside and drew the notebook from his shirt pocket. Uncapped his fountain pen, the one Maman had given him to mark his return from Canada, with his PhD in African History from Laval University. The university which had now, so unexpectedly, offered him a job.

"Well, my children, it is finally happening. We are going to Canada. So tell me. How does it feel?"

"Glorious," said Ludovic, "absolutely glorious."

"I rejoice with you, brother-in-law," Innocent said, "with all of you." He was eager to emigrate as well and Papa had promised to sponsor him once we were settled.

My sister Odile scowled. She was interested in Dieudonné, the son of our neighbours, and she was upset about leaving him behind, although not upset enough to stay.

"Are we going there tomorrow?" Félicité asked. She was only five and didn't understand what we were talking about.

"Not tomorrow, mon trésor, but soon. Very soon. What about you, Domitille, how does it feel to be that much closer to our dream?"

I did not want to emigrate but how could I tell him that? "I'm happy that you're happy," I said instead.

"Clément? Would you like to share your thoughts?"

My brother squirmed on the bench.

Papa recorded all our responses in his notebook, even my brother's squirming. "Now, my second question requires reflection," he paused, as if to show us how. "What will you miss the most about Rwanda?"

We were used to Papa's questions. Interrogations, Clément liked to call them. Our father wanted to know everything. What we were learning at school, what we were doing with our friends, what we were thinking or feeling. This could take a while, as there were five of us, not counting the baby, plus whichever of Maman's brothers and sisters was living with us at the time. That night, there was only Innocent, her youngest brother, as the others had gone to Gitarama for a long visit.

The rules were simple. We didn't have to answer the question (Clément's preference), we had to tell the truth, and we couldn't leave the table until the discussion was over. "I want to know what you think or feel, not what you think I want to hear," Papa was always reminding us.

He also grilled us on current events. *Can the Arusha Accords solve Rwanda's political problems? What will it mean to the rest of Africa once Nelson Mandela is elected president?* Papa knew we weren't interested in the Arusha Accords but he wanted us to think about them anyway, to pay attention to what was happening in our country. As for Nelson Mandela, we couldn't just admire him, we had to consider the broader implications of the coming election in South Africa, the impact it might have on our own country. Not that we could imagine any.

Nyogokuru did not approve of Papa's questions. She thought it was unnatural for him to ask us for our opinion and even more unnatural to write it down. That her son had too much education and not enough sense. Whenever he strayed too far, she would make that clicking sound at the back of her throat and fold her arms under her bosom. Or she would clear the table, making as much noise as possible.

Papa had included Nyogokuru in our application even though she didn't want to emigrate with us. She was eager to return to Kibeho, to live closer to her daughters and her other grandchildren. She had never liked Butare anyway, the university where Papa used to teach, the museum where Maman used to work. Nyogokuru had nothing but contempt for the museum even though one of her prize baskets was on permanent display there.

After Papa lost his job at the university, he drove trucks, dug ditches, wrote letters for people who could not write. Anything to make money. He worked at the boulangerie on Saturday mornings, cursing the dough as he shaped it into baguettes and croissants. Maman, who could no longer work at the museum because she was a Tutsi, taught school in an outlying village.

"What will you miss the most about Rwanda?" Papa repeated, pressing his pen against the page. His smile too bright for the question.

"I miss my Mama," Félicité said.

"I know, sweetness. We all miss your mother very much," Papa said quietly, pausing for a moment before turning to me.

"What about you, Domitille? What will you miss?"

I shrugged. My mind was not on Rwanda but on this Canada, a place we only knew from the postcards Papa had sent home and the photographs he kept at the back of our French dictionary. Photos of stone buildings, busy streets, snow, and a wide blue river.

"Does anyone have an answer ready? What about you, Clément?"

"I'll miss my friends," my twin mumbled.

"Ludovic?"

"Nothing. I shall miss nothing about this country. We can't leave fast enough."

Ludovic hadn't been able to continue his studies because of the restrictions. He worked at the Hôtel Ibis, washing dishes, saving his wages. As single-minded as Papa about this move to Canada.

Papa turned to me again. "Domitille? Will you be answering this question or not?"

"How can I know what I will miss when we haven't left yet? When I don't know what this Canada will be like?"

"Just answer the question, sweetness."

It was an impossible question. I would miss everybody. My best friend, Espérance. My grandmother (not that I believed we'd leave without her). Albertine. All my cousins. My aunts and uncles.

"I will miss Nyogokuru," I finally answered, raising my voice so that my grandmother would hear me over the clatter she was making as she cleared the table. Her face softened but only for a moment.

"I'll miss your endless questions, dear brother-in-law," Innocent offered with a laugh.

"I will miss our families, our country, the beauty of our hills," Maman said.

We were crouching under the banana tree, Papa and I. Everyone else was still asleep. We had our eye on the darkened chrysalis above our heads. I wanted to touch it and see if it was as hard as Tante Célestine's belly, just before her baby was born, but Papa pulled my hand back.

"You must not touch it, sweetness," he whispered, as if the butterfly were sleeping instead of trying to be born.

We waited and waited. We could hear Nyogokuru in the yard now, chasing the evil spirits away, her voice sharp against the quiet. We would've liked to stretch our legs but were afraid to catch her eye. She would've scolded us, laughed in that dismissive way she had, if she had discovered us in the banana grove waiting for a butterfly to be born.

The chrysalis finally moved. Papa held me closer. "Her time has come, sweetness, her time has come." He was still whispering.

The chrysalis shuddered. Once. Twice. Then it cracked open and the butterfly tumbled out, her black-edged blue wings still tucked together, her thin legs grasping the empty sac.

She dangled there for a long time, shifting constantly to keep from falling.

"She's stuck, Papa. We have to help her."

"No, sweetness. Her wings have to fill up and then dry. If you come back in a few hours, you'll be able to see her fly away. Now, I must go or I'll be late for my first class."

Papa crept out of the grove, dusted himself off, picked up the brief-case he had hidden in the low-lying leaves and started walking down the road. I crouched again and cupped my hands under the dangling butterfly so I could catch her if she fell down before her wings were ready.

Even when Papa was still teaching history at the National University, we lived in Ngoma, in a mud brick house with a corrugated roof. Many of his colleagues lived in fancier houses in Buye but Papa wanted to save every franc he could for our emigration. We lived on the ridge, with a view of the valley below, our house shielded from the road by a banana grove.

Nyogokuru was the best basket-weaver in Kibeho. She came to live with us after Grandfather died, bringing all her baskets, some dating back to the time before her marriage. When Maman tried to arrange them, Grandmother lined them up against the wall, muttering that our house was not a museum, that museums were an invention of the *Abazungu* and contrary to our way of life. The comment aimed at Maman who had worked at the National Museum as a curator when it first opened, who had been sent to Belgium for special training.

As soon as Papa accepted the offer in Canada, Nyogokuru started to work on baskets for Odile and me. "We might not have room to bring them with us," Papa warned her. "Why not wait until each girl is ready to be married and send her an *agaseke* as a wedding gift? Or better yet, move with us to Canada."

She had already sorted through her bundles of papyrus leaves and collected the banana flowers and *urukamgi* to make the black and red dyes. I watched her as she coiled the first rows on Odile's basket, the way she sat forward on the three-legged stool Grandfather had made for her. I followed her movements so I could store them in my heart. I couldn't imagine leaving her behind and I was upset with Papa for not doing more to convince her to come with us.

I was known as the invisible one. As a child, I could melt into a shadowy corner, disappear behind a bag of sorghum, vanish under a table. Everyone assumed I was shy but I just wanted to be alone. Our house sheltered seven to ten people, depending on how many of Maman's brothers and sisters were living with us at the time. We sat three to a bench at school. You couldn't walk in any direction without someone greeting you or making a fuss over you or asking a question you didn't wish to answer.

My twin brother (even in my mother's belly I was not alone) used to follow me everywhere. Always asking me what I was doing, where I was going, a habit he never completely outgrew. I continued to hide. In the banana grove in front of the house, in the grassy gullies along the ridge, in the jacarandas behind the school.

One day when I was avoiding walking home with Clément, I stepped through a gap in the orange bougainvillea that lined the ridge. As my feet sank in a freshly-tilled field, my nose filled with the sweet, sharp smell of the earth, my ears with the song of the men who were working their way down the steep slope. Every centimetre of the hill was under cultivation – it was a wonder they didn't tear down the bougainvillea and plough up the road.

As I stepped back through the gap, I noticed remnants of a wall trapped in a tangle of branches and roots. A low wall which had probably been built to prevent the road from washing out in the heavy rains. I was able to track stone in the undergrowth for more than sixty metres.

The next day I returned with Clément's knife – which I had borrowed without asking. The canopy closest to the road was thick and heavy, almost touching the ground, and I was careful not to disturb it. There were a few gaps in the undergrowth but only one wide enough for me to crawl through. I broke off branches and pulled up roots as I went along. Once I reached the wall, I stripped the branches that clung to the stone so I could lean against it.

I heard voices on the road and as they moved closer, I saw feet and the hems of several *pagnes*. There was one voice I recognized, that of a nosy neighbour my grandmother was feuding with. I didn't think anyone could see me but I sat still anyway until the voices drifted out of range.

This soon became my favourite hiding place. I loved the way it glowed orange and smelled sweet. A good place to ponder Papa's questions, to watch and listen to people on the road, to spend time with Espérance. We would whisper and laugh together, our knees touching, our breaths mingling.

We stalled as long as we could. Ludovic described his football match, exaggerating the score to make the game sound more exciting while Odile talked about the wedding preparations for Dieudonné's sister. I recited the poem I was studying at school. Papa listened patiently but he was waiting to pose one of his serious questions – we could tell by the set of his shoulders, the way he was leaning over his notebook.

"Now that the euphoria has died down, we need to consider our decision. To make absolutely sure that we understand what we're doing."

We would've groaned, had we dared. Nyogokuru was already rattling the dishes.

"What is there to understand?" Ludovic asked.

"The enormity of what we're doing. The loved ones we'll be leaving behind. The country that will no longer be our country."

"I no longer consider Rwanda my country," Ludovic said.

"What about you, Odile? What are your thoughts?"

Odile was hemming my school uniform. She pulled the needle through a few more times before she looked up.

"I don't know, Papa. I don't think about Rwanda at all. It's our country, it's where we live, what is there to think about?"

"What about you, Domitille?"

"A country is just an idea, isn't it? The sky, the sun, the trees, the rivers, the animals are blind to the borders that separate us from other countries like Burundi, the Congo, Uganda. So what you're asking is how loyal I am to the idea of our country."

"You surprise me, Domitille. What have you been reading?"

"She's been listening to Monsieur Nzeyimana," Clément muttered. Monsieur Nzeyimana was our history teacher and my brother didn't like his questions any more than he did Papa's.

"Ah. The teacher who dares to teach *amateka*." Papa said, "Who has yet to learn that history is an impossible subject in this country."

"It's our country that's impossible."

"Yes, I know how you feel, Ludovic. Now does anyone else have a question, a comment?"

"Who is Euphoria and how did she die?" Félicité wanted to know.

We all laughed, even Nyogokuru, only her eyes were bright with tears.

I stood at the back of our new classroom while others scrambled to claim their seats. Clément had already claimed his, the one furthest from the teacher and closest to the door. He'd sprinted ahead to secure that spot, the only day of the year he hurried to school.

The bench I wanted was already occupied by two people. At our other school, the one we'd outgrown, the front row bench was always the last to be taken. Even the eager students didn't wish to sit under the teacher's nose like I did. The classroom was the only place where I didn't try to hide.

I took the last place on the bench. The girl on my left turned, her smile so bright it startled me.

"Domitille," I whispered, as if my name were a secret.

"Espérance," she whispered back.

Monsieur Nzeyimana never opened his history textbook but carried it with him while he walked around the classroom. Like a talisman. He was young, handsome, and full of enthusiasm. Didn't teach like any professor we knew.

He usually started our lesson with a story. An article in the newspaper. An inflammatory speech on *Radio Milles Collines*. An account of the Virgin Mary's appearance in Kibeho. One of the Royal myths.

"History is a basket," he would often tell us. "You can put everything in it. The past, the present, the exploits of our ancestors, our everyday lives."

That day, he recited the beginning of the Gihanga myth as he stood at the back of the class.

"Gihanga is the son of Kazi, the son of Kizira, the son of Gisa, the son of Randa, the son of Merano, the son of Koobo, the son of Kimanuka, the son of Kijuru, the son of Muntu, the son of Kigwa, the son of Nkuba, who is Shyerezo."

I closed my eyes. His voice was as thick and sweet as his lips and each name sounded like it had been kissed.

"You are all familiar with this, yes? You've heard it many times. But have you ever really thought about it? What it means?"

"Why does it have to mean anything?"

"All the myths start that way. With a list of ascendants."

"A boring list."

"Yes, very boring."

"I like the rhythm of it."

"And what can rhythm do?"

"Help us remember the names?"

"But it's a list of mythological kings!"

"This is not history."

"Isn't it?"

His voice was very close now. I opened my eyes to find him in front of me, his elegant hands gesticulating between us.

"Myths can tell us a lot about our ancestors, how they lived, what was important to them. The lists of ascendants, which you find so boring, taught them how to record their history, starting with the names of their own kings and chiefs. The myth-telling, the oral tradition that grew out of it, and the history we are learning today are all related."

Monsieur Nzeyimana looked at me as he said this. Did he know my Papa could no longer teach history at the university because he was a Tutsi? Was he worried that he might lose his own job for the same reason?

As I walked home, I wondered about the myths we'd have to learn in Canada and the restrictions we'd face once we moved there.

Corentin was howling. I took him outside before he disturbed Maman who had been up with him all night. The baby was so heavy now I could barely carry him and squirming so much I was afraid

I would drop him. When I walked around the house a few times, as Nyogokuru would've done, he howled even louder. The sunbirds in the banana grove responded with a noisy outburst of their own. Maman came to find us, the exhaustion etched on her face.

"He misses his mother," she said as she took him from me.

A mother he had never known, who died at his birth. When Corentin and Félicité became part of our family, our emigration was delayed by several months. Canada wanted more documentation, a declaration of consent from their father. But everything had been arranged and now Papa had an offer of employment from Laval University.

Maman started to hum and sway. She pressed the baby's head gently into her shoulder and whenever he lifted it again to scream, she pressed it back. Her humming was loud now, her swaying more pronounced. I could feel the words rising in her throat.

Nkwihoreze ibyandango ayiwe, ayiwe
ibyandongo, nkwihoreze ikobondo humm,
humm, ayiwe ayiwe, ibyandongo
hora hora shenge ayiwe ayiwe
ibyandongo, nkubwire uduhoza abana humm

I will console you, my baby
Get rid of your sorrow, my little one, my little chick.
Don't cry, don't cry, my heart
I will sing you the most beautiful lullabies, my treasure

Corentin cried as if he could not forgive us for being alive when his own mother was dead. Maman handed me the baby and took me in her arms, Corentin between us. We swayed from side to side. I sang with Maman.

Nta joro wandaje ayiwe, ayiwe
ibyandongo, amanywas, umugoroba humm

The nights are calm by your side, my baby
The days and the evenings, by your side, my littlest one.

At home, we had been taught to identify ourselves as Rwandans, as Africans, not as Tutsi. Papa was adamant about it. At school, the reality was different. Especially at our new school where most of the students and teachers were Hutu (forgive me, Papa). Monsieur Nzeyimana was the only Tutsi teacher left and Abondance and his friends disrupted his history class every day and never missed an opportunity to insult those of us who were Tutsi (forgive me again, Papa). Abondance had everything, as his name suggested: intelligence, good looks, and talent. Everything but tolerance.

Monsieur Nzeyimana refused to be intimidated and continued to weave whatever happened to us into the history of our country. One afternoon, he started the lesson without a story, without reading anything. He pulled down a map we had never seen before. Old and tattered.

"Can anyone show me where Nyanza is?"

"Nyabisindu," Abondance interrupted.

"Yes, it has been renamed Nyabisindu but on this old map it's still labelled Nyanza, which is what it was called at the time of the *Abami*. And since we're going to talk about the Abami today, about the last days of the Tutsi kings–"

"We don't want to hear about the Tutsi kings. We don't want to hear about the *inyenzi*!"

Inyenzi. Cockroaches.

"I've warned you before, Abondance, not to use that word in my classroom."

"I am being historically accurate. *Abami* then, *inyenzi* now"

His friends laughed. Those who were afraid of Abondance laughed as well.

"You had better leave and report to the principal."

The boy crossed his arms, stayed where he was. When Espérance slid off our bench and approached him, he smiled. He was attracted to her. All the boys were. She leaned over and seemed about to kiss him. She bit his nose instead.

"Cockroaches bite. Remember that."

He grabbed his nose but no one dared laugh. When Espérance returned to our bench, she gripped my hand. I could feel her whole body shaking. How brave she was.

The teacher pointed to the map again. "Now, can someone show me where Nyanza is?"

No one stirred. I wanted to be brave, to walk up to the map and point to the town, but I was scared of Abondance and his friends. *Amateka* is important, Papa always said, but it's like walking into a swamp, never knowing if you will be able to walk out again.

Maman taught school in a village on the next ridge and it took her more than an hour to walk home. I often went to meet her halfway, at the bottom of our hill. I loved this time alone with Maman, without Corentin hanging around her neck or Nyogokuru complaining about the neighbours, the price of sorghum, or the foreigners she had seen in town.

"What was Belgium like?" I asked her one day, as we trudged up our hill. The dread about our move to Canada rooted deep in my heart.

"I don't know, sweetness. I spent the four months of my training in Tervuren and never even saw Brussels, except for the airport. You should ask your Papa, he lived there for two years."

"I know all of Papa's stories. I wanted to know what it was like for you."

She sighed. "I was there in the winter. It was cold and damp. We only had four months to learn what was usually taught over a year."

"And the people? What were they like?"

"Some were kind."

"And the others?"

"Not as much."

"Was there snow?"

"Sometimes. But mostly cold rain."

She slowed down when we reached the next bend of the road. Where you could see across to the school where she taught. It was nothing more than a shed, really.

"Do you like teaching at that school?"

"The children are eager to learn."

"Do you miss working at the museum?"

"I don't think about the past."

Not like Papa. I had seen him more than once walk to the university where he could no longer teach, his briefcase in hand as if he still worked there. Or sitting in the kitchen with one of his history textbooks, writing notes in the margin, erasing others.

We stopped again when we reached our ridge. This was my favourite time of the day. The hills huddling together as darkness approached, the trees like cutouts against the deep red of the sky.

I found Clément in my hiding place one Saturday. I rarely went there on that day because I had to help Nyogokuru sell her baskets at the market.

"What are you doing here?" he asked.

"What am *I* doing here? This is my hiding place."

"The bougainvillea belongs to everyone and you cleared this space using my knife so I have as much right as you to be here."

I didn't respond. I didn't want to argue. Not here, in this place.

I stared at him without speaking which I knew would drive him crazy. He started to squirm almost immediately. The more he squirmed, the stiller I became. Nyogokuru believed our spirits had not separated properly at birth, that we were extremes of each other. It was her explanation for everything. Why I wanted to be alone and Clément always wanted to be with people. Why I loved school and he hated it. Why he fidgeted so much and I was always calm.

He sighed. Rubbed his head and face in one motion, the way monkeys do.

"How long have you known about this place?" I finally asked.

"Since the day you borrowed my knife."

"From the beginning then?"

It was my turn to sigh. "Why have you been coming here? When you don't like to sit still and there's nothing to do here but sit still."

"I want to feel what you feel when you come here."

"But how can you feel what I feel when we are so different?"

"Why don't you love me? Why are you always running away from me?"

"I do love you, Clément. You're my brother. And I run away from everyone."

"Not Espérance."

"Yes, even Espérance. She has been here five or six times. I come here almost every day."

"The wall is cursed, you know. Something bad happened here."

"Who told you this?"

"I heard Nyogokuru and a woman talking about it last week. They were both crying."

"What woman?"

"I don't know who she is. I've never seen her before. They embraced and talked about what a sad day it was, how that wall should never have been built, and then went down the road together."

"Are you sure they were talking about this wall?"

He nodded. Rubbed his head and face again.

We stayed a little while longer and then we walked home. Arm in arm.

I could not stop thinking about the wall. About what might have happened there. When I finally asked Nyogokuru, her face darkened, her eyes hardened.

"Don't even mention that wall to me."

"But I only want to know—"

She picked up her stool and the basket she was weaving for Odile and went outside. I turned to my father who was sitting at the kitchen table reading an old newspaper he had found.

"What happened to that wall?"

He glanced outside where Nyogokuru had resumed her weaving. Folded his newspaper. Let out a long sigh.

"The commune was building a wall to prevent the road from washing away in the rains," he told me in a voice so low I could barely hear him. "Three of the workers were killed, the only Tutsi on the project, including my brother Auguste who was seventeen."

He got up, looked out the window, and sat down again.

"Auguste had never worked in construction before but he was tall and strong. When he asked me to recommend him to the foreman of the project, a childhood friend of mine, I urged him to stay in school but he wouldn't listen. I passed his name on to the foreman who hired him and two of his friends."

He stopped. Clenched his hands.

"They were killed after a month, bludgeoned against the wall they were building. Their pay envelopes still in their pockets. My father came down from Kibeho in a drunken rage. He went to the police but they told him to sober up and come back the next day. When he stormed into the prefecture, he was quickly escorted from the building. Undeterred, he waited outside, hoping to catch an official on his way in or out. When someone left a truck idling just inside the gate, he climbed into it and drove to the construction site. It was deserted but there were banana pickers working along the ridge, he could hear them singing. He rammed the wall anyway. By the time the police arrived, he had already knocked down a whole section. He climbed out of the truck and let it roll down the hill, ruining part of the crop and scattering those who were working there. Luckily no one was hurt."

"But Grandfather was so kind and gentle."

"He was neither. By the time you knew him, he was a broken man. He spent two years in prison for damaging the truck, the wall and the crop. Those who killed his son were never prosecuted, never punished."

"Stand still."

Since we were the same height and build, Odile was using me to adjust the dress she was making with material Dieudonné's sister had given her. A dress my parents didn't approve of because she was entering it in a contest. A contest they didn't want her to win.

"I'm sure you'll win, Odile. You're so clever with the needle."

"It's sweet of you to think so, little sister, but Madame Mugiraneza doesn't like me. I can't win."

"What do you mean?"

"The contest isn't real, Domitille. She'll pick the girl she wants and seem magnanimous at the same time."

"I don't understand."

"Madame Mugiraneza is the best seamstress in Butare. Every mother in town wants to apprentice her daughter to her, except Maman, of course, who doesn't appreciate her skills. By holding a so-called contest, Madame makes it look like every girl has a fair chance at winning the apprenticeship. Now turn to your left."

"Why are you entering the contest then?"

"Because I love to sew."

She started pinning the hem again and humming.

Odile wanted to work as a seamstress in Kigali but our parents wanted her to finish school. Nyogokuru, who thought education was wasted on girls, had encouraged her to enter the contest.

Nyogokuru arrived just as I stepped down from the bench. She set her basket on the table and asked me to turn slowly in front of her. When I stopped, she checked the buttonholes, the darts at the waist, the hem, the seams. Without saying anything, without complaining about the dress being foreign. Odile was still humming as she emptied the basket, a French tune that was popular at the time on the radio.

I walked by my hiding place every day without stopping or even slowing down. Only my eyes lingered on the bougainvillea blossoms, on the stone that lurked in the undergrowth.

When Espérance asked me why I was avoiding it, I didn't explain, didn't tell her about Auguste. Nyogokuru and Papa's secret was now my secret. Maybe my uncle's *abazima* had led me to the wall, maybe he wanted me to keep his soul company.

One Sunday, when I was looking for one of Nyogokuru's goats, I found myself on that stretch of road. I had just reached the low branches that masked the entrance to my hiding place when I heard the goat bleat somewhere behind me. I stood still, waiting for him to bleat again, but he had already bounded away.

I heard someone laugh. It was Abondance. No one else laughed like that. The way a snake would, if it could. Quick and furtive. I looked up the road although I knew it had come from under the bougainvillea. The road was empty. It was Sunday morning and most people were in church.

"Cockroaches bite. Remember that!"

It was Espérance's voice.

They were making other sounds now. Sounds I recognized. I lifted a branch and started to creep forward. They were getting so noisy they wouldn't hear me, even if a twig snapped. It took a while for my eyes to adjust. There was enough light coming in that I could make out their naked bodies. I could see Abondance's long legs, the curve of his bum. One of Espérance's breasts. They were moving together on my grandmother's straw mat, the one I had taken from the shed without her permission.

I was ashamed that Espérance had brought this boy, who had called us *inyenzi*, to my secret place so that they could lie together. Against the wall where my uncle died because he was a Tutsi, although she had no way of knowing that. The more I watched them, the more shame I felt, the more my womanly parts burned with desire.

Espérance realized that I knew when I sat beside her the next morning. When I shrank from her touch as she put her hands on my shoulders and rubbed her forehead against mine.

"Oh, sweetness," was all she could say.

I didn't wait for her at the end of the day so she ran after me. Grabbed my hands and held them against her bosom.

"I wanted to tell you, Domitille, but I was afraid of how you would react. I didn't plan for this to happen. It just did."

"But it's Abondance. The boy who called us cockroaches in class."

"I know. Please don't hate me. I couldn't stand it if you hated me."

"I saw you. In our private place…"

I couldn't look at her.

"We have nowhere else to go."

"And I thought you were so brave. Going up to him and biting his nose like that!"

We continued to share the same bench at school but we no longer walked home together. There was distance between us now. Like she lived on one hill and I on another.

I dribbled mango juice on my cousin's face, her chubby little arms and legs. She sat perfectly still, following my every move with her big brown eyes. Félicité was a quiet child, slows to smile, in spite of her name. I dribbled juice on my face and arms and stretched out under the banana tree, my sticky hands palms up. She lay down too, resting her head on my belly.

We sang while we waited for the butterflies to land on us but softly so Clément wouldn't hear us and spoil our fun. My brother loved butterflies but he was only interested in counting and identifying them. He made fun of the names I gave them. Names like Amaranthe and Célimène and Églantine. "They can't hear you," he'd remind me scornfully, when he caught me talking to them, "they don't have ears."

Papa often called me his little butterfly, his little kinyugunyugu.

A butterfly landed on Félicité's nose. Two others landed on her forehead and another on her cheek while others hovered over her head. I soon had some on my nose, my cheeks, and my lips. Their tiny legs dancing on my skin, their wings scattering orange and yellow shadows over my face. I closed my eyes and held my breath to listen to the sound of their wings but all I could hear was Félicité's breathing and the beating of my heart.

Ludovic was watching me feed the chickens. I could see his motorcycle on the road, just beyond the banana grove. It wasn't really his motorcycle, it belonged to his friend Emmanuel who had fled to Uganda. Ludovic had not ridden it for months, saving the money he would have otherwise spent on petrol for our pending emigration.

"I'm taking you for a ride," he announced as I flung the last of the grain from the bowl.

I stepped back. Shook my head. I was the only person in the family who had never ridden on it. Even Nyogokuru had let him take her into town a few times.

"It's your last chance. Emmanuel has asked me to bring it to his uncle in Mbazi."

"How can it be my last chance when I never wanted one in the first place?"

Ludovic laughed off my question and took the bowl from my hand. Dropped it in the sack of grain. "Come."

I followed him reluctantly. He climbed on the bike and I hoisted myself behind him as I had seen Espérance hoist herself on Abondance's motorbike after school. He rode back and forth on our road so I would get used to the motion before he tackled the hill.

"Ready?"

I pressed my face against his damp shirt, closed my eyes. Held him tight. I would have liked to sit like Espérance, head high, back straight, my arms linked loosely around his waist. A smile on my lips. But I was too afraid.

I screamed as we hurtled down the hill. My fear only lessening when we arrived at the bottom and the road levelled out. My body aligned itself with my brother's, our bodies with the bike. The road was paved and I wondered if the French had paved it. What was the point of building these beautiful roads when almost everyone travelled on foot? When children went hungry? When they could not be spared to go to school? Even on a motorbike, kilometres from home, Papa's voice was in my head.

When we started to climb again, I tightened my grip and closed my eyes, praying that we would not tumble down the hill and break Papa's heart. We stopped on the ridge.

"How much farther?" I asked, hoping he had taken a detour and that we wouldn't have to walk all that way back.

He shrugged.

"I love this time of the day," he said, as he folded his long legs and settled on the ground. "The way the light hangs above the hills like a fine mist."

"I thought you weren't going to miss anything about Rwanda."

"I won't miss Rwanda, no matter how beautiful her hills are."

"Are there hills in Canada?"

He laughed. "Of course there are hills in Canada. There are also mountains and plains and vast forests, lakes that are bigger than Lake Kivu, many rivers. Glaciers. Even a desert. Canada is more than 350 times the size of our country."

"I've never been further than Gitarama. I don't know my own country so how can I imagine one that is 350 times bigger?"

"You don't have to. You'll only live in a small corner of it, just like you live in a small corner of Rwanda now. And it will become familiar and eventually feel like home."

I was not so sure.

As we looked down into a valley much like our own, I tried to imagine the hills in Canada. With snow on them. There was snow in Rwanda, high up in the mountains, but I had never seen it.

Albertine walked to the other side of the table and settled on the bench closer to the radio. Nyogokuru glared at her for being so restless. I glanced out the window, worried that Papa would come home and catch us listening to the Pope's address. He was at his office at the university, marking papers. Maman was at the market with Odile and I could hear Clément and his friends outside.

Papa had railed against the Pope's visit. Blaming the Catholic Church for keeping Rwanda overpopulated and poor. Maman and Papa didn't believe in God but had us baptized so we could attend Catholic schools. I went to mass with Nyogokuru sometimes, just to keep her company.

There was static and then a long silence. Were we going to miss it altogether?

"Chers amis, paysans du Rwanda," the Pope finally began. Albertine clapped her hands softly. "I would like to climb your hills, look over your fields, be welcomed in your homes, but my visit to your country is too brief to allow it..." I liked his voice, the sound of his French.

Albertine and Nyogokuru both looked as if God were speaking to them directly.

"Thanks to you, Rwanda is moving forward. You are responsible for this progress, through your hard work, the yield of your fields... I know the many difficulties you face..."

I had expected him to talk about God but he was talking about unfavourable economic conditions, just like Papa would.

"It is up to you to take charge of your own development. It is important that you know how to organize, to make yourself heard."

Still no mention of God. Nyogokuru was frowning. Albertine had her eyes closed, that smile she always had when she was praying.

The Pope talked about freedom and justice. Why was Papa not here to listen to this? Why didn't he know that the Pope was on our side? Only towards the end, did he mention the Gospels, speak of Jesus. "May He bless you and accompany you in your daily toil. May he keep alive your hope for a better world."

Nyogokuru turned the radio off and started to prepare dinner. Albertine came to sit beside me and squeezed my hand. She was my mother's sister but so close to me in age I didn't call her Tante. She had lived with us since she was six and had remained devout in spite of our godless home. She had left us to join the Bénébikira Sisters although my mother had done everything to prevent it.

"I wish I could have gone to Kigali to hear him. To see him with my own eyes."

"I'm glad you came to see us instead. We miss you so much."

"I'm here for a whole month. And you can come and visit me at the convent once I have completed my novitiate."

"And how long is that?"

"Two years."

"I won't be able to see you for two years?"

"It will go quickly. You'll see."

When Papa received his notice to appear at the Canadian consulate in Kigali, he danced around the table again. Took Maman to the Hôtel Ibis to celebrate. Nyogokuru wept the minute they left, pushed me away when I tried to console her.

Within days we were all wailing. The President's plane had been shot down in Kigali and there were reports of widespread killings. My parents were up every night listening to the shortwave radio Papa had brought back from Canada, turning down the sound so we could not hear it.

Maman tried to reassure Papa that as bad as things were in Kigali, we were safe in Butare for now. "The U.N. will not allow this to continue," she kept saying. Which was unusual as Maman was not one to repeat herself.

"We cannot count on the United Nations. No one on the Security Council cares what happens to our country," my father would counter, his eyes more worried than we had ever seen them.

Unfortunately it was Papa who was right. The United Nations' troops pulled out. The news worsened.

Papa retrieved the large backpack he had stored in the shed. It contained dried food packets he had also brought back from Canada, a machete, rope, matches. Maman told us to wear our two sets of clothes, one over the other, so Papa could use the layers to hide cigarettes, Belgian francs, music tapes, anything he could trade with. Maman wore a *pagne* and an *igitambaro* around her head, instead of her modern clothes, the ones Grandmother complained about.

Nyogokuru refused to come with us. "No one is going to bother an old woman like me. Save your children. That is your duty." We embraced her, our kisses sliding off her wet cheeks.

We left in the middle of the night. We were not the only ones on the road but everyone was so quiet we were like an army of ghosts advancing. Maman must've given something to Corentin to keep him quiet. We avoided many roadblocks by walking across fields; slipped by others if the men were sleeping or too drunk to rouse themselves.

Morning arrived before we could reach the border so we hid in a field of sorghum for the rest of the day. We saw men on the road brandishing pangas, their shirts covered in blood, chanting Hutu Power slogans. Maman tried to shield our eyes but did not have enough hands. At midnight we set out again and reached the border crossing just before dawn. There were three thousand people there already, Papa figured. We waited around for two days and on the third day, we set out along the Akanyaru River to find another place to cross.

The river is swollen, fast-moving, the water reddish-brown from sediment. Burundi lies on the other side. It looks no different from here, no safer.

We are hiding in a banana grove. Papa and Ludovic have dug a hole for all of us to hide in, with dried banana leaves woven on a frame to pull over us at the last minute.

Whenever I start to panic, I imagine myself in another place, the orange light on my face, blossoms under my feet. The wall solid against my back. Two of Papa's questions buzz in my brain. *What will you miss the most about Rwanda? What will it mean to the rest of Africa when Nelson Mandela is elected president?* The election is in two weeks. Mandela's victory will come too late for our wretched country.

I will miss Nyogokuru. Who laughs so loudly and regally. Like an umugabekazi.

I will miss Albertine, who is so gentle and good. Who smiles like she has just come down from heaven.

I will miss Espérance, who is so bold and brave. May Abondance protect her.

I will miss my teacher, Monsieur Nzeyimana, who has been so kind to me. Whose lips I have always wanted to kiss.

It is the rainy season so the river will not subside any time soon. Papa is the only one who can swim. He learned to swim in Canada and has promised us swimming lessons in our new country, in a pool inside a building. Maman used to have a postcard of the pool at the Hôtel Meridien in Kigali, where she once worked as a chambermaid.

While Papa and Ludovic hack off eucalyptus branches to make a raft, Clément and I sit on opposite sides of the clearing to listen for anyone approaching. We heard screaming earlier but it is quiet now.

By the time the sun sets, the raft is ready. Papa has decided to ferry us two at a time because he feels the raft is too flimsy to carry us all safely. When Maman protests, he whispers something to her and she recoils. He divides us into pairs: Ludovic and Félicité, Odile and Corentin, Clément and me, and gives us a rendezvous point in the first town on the Burundi side, in case we get separated somehow. We cry as we embrace. Papa sets off with Ludovic and Félicité and disappears into the blackness.

It seems like hours before Papa returns. We are relieved when the raft emerges out of the darkness that is the river and everything around it. He helps Odile onto the raft and when he reaches for the baby, Maman backs away. *"Aurélie, il le faut,"* he pleads softly. Maman weeps as Papa coaxes Corentin out of her arms. As the raft disappears again into the blackness, Clément and I huddle against her and settle in for the wait.

"What did Papa say earlier, when you didn't want us to be divided into pairs?" my brother wants to know. Fidgeting like he always does.

"Nothing important, *mon coeur.* Nothing important."

I was standing close enough to Maman to hear. Papa was afraid the raft would be attacked. That we would all die together. He was trying to even the odds.

We wait and we wait but Papa does not return. Maman starts to weep again, falling on her knees, the way she wept after Tante Pascaline died giving birth to Corentin last year. Pascaline. I remember when she used to live with us. How eager she was to answer Papa's never-ending questions.

I will miss our house in Ngoma.
The baskets in the shed, leaning against each other, their lids askew.
The sunbirds in the banana grove.
The bleating of Nyogokuru's goats.
The lowing of our neighbour's cow.

When dawn breaks, we are still clinging to the hope that Papa was waiting for daylight. We scan the other shore, the river, but there is no sign of the raft. When we finally see something in the water, it's the body of a boy, seven or eight years old. Two more bodies follow, face down. His parents maybe. When several more bodies float by, one of them a baby, Maman falls on her knees again and wails.

"Papa will be back soon," we assure her as we try to block the view of the river. "We should hide under the banana leaves until he comes back."

Maman wipes away her tears and straightens up. "I need to find food. Climb into the hole and wait for your Papa. I saw avocado over there yesterday."

There is still some dried food left but I don't mention it.

When she returns with several avocados and a bunch of bananas as there are no ripe ones in our grove, we force ourselves to eat, our backs to the river where the bodies are so thick we could walk across. There are several other families hiding out along the river now but we don't speak to them. The bodies have already told us everything we need to know.

The day passes and another night.

I will miss the hills, lush and green.
The way the mist lingers on them in the early morning.
The way they soften and blur just before the sun goes down.

"I will have to swim across," Maman announces as we wipe the sleep from our eyes. There is no mist on the river this morning. No bodies floating by.

"But we don't have a raft," my brother says.

"I will take you one at a time. You first, Clément, then I will come back for Domitille. It is our only hope."

"But you don't know how to swim!"

I want to protest too but the words scurry down my throat. Hide in my lungs. Make it difficult for me to breathe.

"Yes, I do. I learned to swim when I worked at the Hôtel Méridien in Kigali. I never told your Papa."

"But why?"

"Because he didn't know how to swim then. Because he would've hated the man who taught me."

The man must have been French or Belgian.

"That was a long time ago, Maman. Maybe you've forgotten how."

"Non, Clément. I swam every day when I was in Belgium. Our hotel didn't have a piscine but there was an indoor pool at the community centre. Swimming is what kept me sane. We need to set out now. The sooner we leave, the sooner I can come back for Domitille."

"I will come back. I promise," she whispers to me.

She knows I'm braver than Clément, that he'll panic if she takes me first, so I don't protest. We hug each other for a long time. Clément has wet himself, I can smell it.

I try to be brave, like Espérance. Where is she now? Is she safe?

Maman rolls up her *pagne* and ties the ends so that her legs are free. She wades out into the river and when she tries to get Clément to float on his back, he only flails in the water. She whispers something to him and they try again. And again. Maybe taking Clément first is not a good idea.

Finally, he lies on his back without flailing. He looks over at me, his eyes wide with fear, and I smile at him. The most encouraging smile I can muster.

Maman slips one arm under his, makes sure he is hanging on and starts to swim. I'm surprised at how well she swims, better than Papa, it seems to me. The current is strong and although they are making steady progress, it soon carries them out of sight. I run along the shore until I can no longer see them. I trudge back to the empty banana grove to wait.

The day passes slowly.
Maman does not return.
I'm hiding in the hole, the frame of banana leaves overhead.

Night falls.
I don't sleep.
I hear screaming far away.

The sun rises.
Maman still has not returned.

I walk along the shore until I reach the point where I lost sight of them.

Burundi is still so close. Still so far.

I pray for Maman and Papa. Ludovic, Odile, and Clément. Félicité and Corentin. Imagine them safe and together on the other side of the river. Papa and Ludovic working on a new raft, waiting until night fall to come and get me.

I pray for Nyogokuru and Albertine. For Maman's brothers and sisters, Célestine, Gaspard, Hugolin, and Innocent. For all our cousins in Gitarama.

I pray for Papa's sisters, Delphine, Bérénice and Elvire. For our many cousins in Kibeho.

I pray for Espérance and Monsieur Nzeyimana.

It's only when I try to pray for myself that I falter.

I may be Rwandan, I may be African, but I will die a Tutsi. Forgive me, Papa.

Abami (pl. of Mwami)	Tutsi kings
abazima	soul
Abazungu (pl. of Umuzungu)	foreigner, white person
agaseke	covered basket
amateka	history
Arusha Accords	agreement for sharing political power within Rwanda
igitambaro	traditional head covering
isombe	stew of cassava leaves, eggplant, peppers and onions
Kibeho	schoolgirls in this town reported seeing the Virgin Mary in the 1980s
Nyogokuru	paternal grandmother
pagne	traditional dress
panga	machete
Radio Milles Collines	private radio and television station that disseminated hate propaganda against the Tutsi
umugabekazi	queen
urukamgi	a plant whose roots and seeds are boiled to make red dye

ACKNOWLEDGEMENTS

These are some of the books that inspired and guided me in the creation of this work:

Long Shadows: Truth, Lies and History by Erna Paris, *A Chorus of Stones: The Private Life of War* by Susan Griffin, *Regarding the Pain of Others* by Susan Sontag, and *Identity and Violence: The Illusion of Destiny* by Amartya Sen

The Specter of Genocide: Mass Murder in Historical Perspective, edited by Robert Gellately and Ben Kiernan

The Young Turks' Crime Against Humanity: The Armenian Genocide and Ethnic Cleansing in the Ottoman Empire by Taner Akçam and *Survivors: an Oral History of the Armenian Genocide* by Donald E. Miller and Lorna Touryan Miller

The Harvest of Sorrow: Soviet Collectivization and the Terror-Famine by Robert Conquest and *Execution by Hunger: The Hidden Holocaust*, a personal account by Simon Starow (writing under the pseudonym Miron Dolot)

The Rape of Nanking: The Forgotten Holocaust of World War II by Iris Chang and the novel *Nanjing 1937: A Love Story* by Ye Zhaoyan

La Shoah en France (4 volumes) by Serge Klarsfeld, *Journal 1942-1944* by Hélène Berr, and *Les enfants du silence: Mémoires d'enfants cachés 1939-45* by Jean-Marie Guéno

The Pol Pot Regime: Race, Power, and Genocide in Cambodia under the Khmer Rouge, 1975-79 by Ben Kiernan and *When Broken Glass Floats* by Chanrithy Him

The Rwanda Crisis: History of a Genocide by Gérard Prunier and *N'aie pas peur de savoir: Rwanda : un million de morts, une rescapée tutsi raconte* by Yolande Mukagasana

You will find an extensive bibliography as well as maps, photos, and video clips at www.lysechampagne.ca.

I owe thanks to so many people, especially:

Gregg Shilliday, Catharina de Bakker, Mel Marginet, and Ingeborg Boyens at Great Plains Publications, for taking a chance on this project. For their enthusiasm and good humour.

The amazing staff at the Ottawa Public Library.

Professor Isabel Kaprelian-Churchill, Professor Bert Vaux, Monsieur Jean-Patrick Charrey, Ms. Jo-Ann Gloger, Mr. Pavlo Dyban and Monsieur Jean Baptiste Mugiraneza, for answering my many questions.

Madame Lucie Caulliveau, for sharing her memories of the Occupation in the French village of Méaudre, in Quatre-Montagnes (now known as the Vercors).

Kim Jernigan, former editor of *The New Quarterly*, for her valuable feedback on four of the stories and for publishing my earlier work.

The editors who published shorter versions of three stories from this collection. One Step at a Time is Good Walking appeared in *Descant* in 2010; Mal'achim in *The New Quarterly* in 2009; and On the Bank of the Akanyaru River in *The Toronto Star* in 2005.

Didier Jeunesse (Paris) for *Les Plus Belles Berceuses du Monde: 23 berceuses du Mali au Japon* in which I found the Rwandan lullaby (the translation from the French is mine).

My first readers, for their comments and encouragement: Rick Kenny, Anne Douglas, Russ Hawley, Michèle Champagne, Sharon Knapp, Caroline Whitby, Carol Michon, Rosemary Leach, Sheilagh Keelan, Helen Lynn, Nancy Smyth, Barbara Clubb, and Dorothy Speak.

Alexis, Marieke, Saskia, Mélisande, Kim, Jordana, and Kaiya for bringing such joy to my life.

Rick for his unwavering love and support.